"Russell Persson does with Cabeza de Vaca's narrative what Nick Cave did with traditional murder ballads: hones it, gives it a sharp edge, and makes it seem almost uncomfortably close. An incantatory and compelling read, one that will stick with you long after the book is closed."

BRIAN EVENSON

"Persson, God, where does one begin? There is a seriousness to the pages of Russell Persson that is rarely seen in this age of the instantaneous. Read Persson closely and you will see that he is extremely defiant. He is also extremely subtle in his defiance."

DAVID MCLENDON

"*The Way of Florida* is a compact, driving, rhythmical work … complex, rich, sinuous – a novel, but quite unlike most."

TOM JEFFREYS

"Russell Persson has writerly lungs of brass; his great long, taut and deep sentences run by river fast but aren't just shape but meaning and mystery both."

DAVID HAYDEN

THE WAY OF FLORIDA

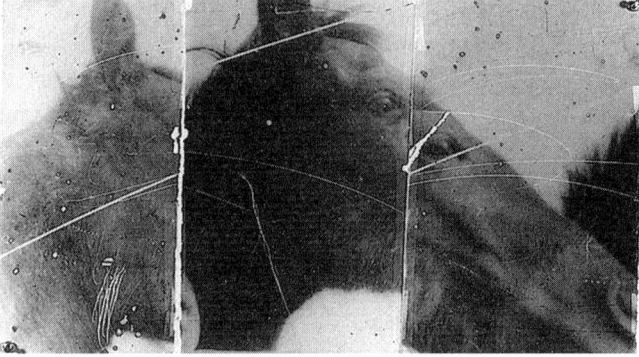

FICTIONS

THE WAY OF FLORIDA

A Novel
by Russell Persson

LITTLE ISLAND PRESS

Lodgemore Lane,
Stroud, GL5 3EQ

Published in the United Kingdom by
Little Island Press, Stroud

© Russell Persson, 2017

Frontispiece © Doug and Mike Starn, 2017

ISBN 978-0-9957052-0-3

Series design by t.r.u
typographic research unit

Typeset in Bembo MT
Printed and bound in Great Britain by TJ International

CONTENTS

To Katie and to my Mother and Father

THE WAY OF FLORIDA

I

And waiting another day to enter port, a south wind took us and drove us away from land. We passed over to the coast of Florida, and came to land, and went along the coast the way of Florida.

Lone flats due east of Dry Tortuga, the shallows there. The pilot ran us aground for all he knows. Four hundred men and eighty horses and four ships and brigantine. High up on this shoal in spring the groans of us and the groans our ship does against its own damn weight. The groans and walking, only stillness could break them down. If I hear another man pace today this pilot who shoaled us up here answers for that sound I swear. Hardtack and water barreled and a fruit destroyed inside it for its medicine against a worm. Dry Tortuga far out and east of us the bonefish in between. The fish in clouds around us.

Then it was the cloth of our Lord commanded our silence and I along with the great wishes of our keeper gone along with this for any bend in the ritual of our pause there run aground was itself a gift and so it must have been what our Lord intended for us that great heads of rain walked over us and our grounded ship inside this sea above the sea was for now a quiet one save what fell against the decks from it. We couldn't help but give ourselves to what it was and stare out through its curtain of falls. We had a sea around us is what I said. The horse can subdue itself if about them a peace is made, like any other beast, and so it was. The damp horse still and headhung close up against so all eighty head and hide are blended into one. What steadies us here though is the water pourn I'm certain of it. Our Lord is quiet boots upon man I know this at least.

Sat there for two fucking weeks. Blown by three storms since Havana. This pilot of the north coast, Miruelo. I have a time constructing words to go with him.

Our doldrum broken, we went along the coast of Florida. Then we anchored on the same coast at the mouth of a bay. Across the bay we saw buhios and where Indians live.

Like a waypoint an island in the bay was our halfshot and each met there, the Indians who paddled there in dugout canoes and our comptroller Alonso Enriquez and some men with him rowed there in a skiff. The Indians brought with them fish and venison and they were with Enriquez for the day on that island. And after they left the island they paddled in their canoes back across the bay and in the night they gathered all they had and lit some cookfires that we saw from across the bay and what they gathered was hauled out with them and they disappeared into the night trees so that when we arrived the next day their buhios were empty and a great buhio that could hold three hundred of them was bare of them entire. Some of them must have gone coasted, oversea in canoes so all canoes were gone. Among it all we found a golden rattle.

And standing on this cleared town this land is presented to his royal name and orders as commanded.

Of our horses the sick and thin horse is all who remained. Half of what started, so many dead and brought up and dropped into the waves and sunk overboard, falling dead in seawater into some depth who makes all souls opaque. One after another. And who remained were thin and worn. My sorrow for the sunken horses I also cannot put words to but for a different why.

And when the Indians returned the next day with their language that they used into our ears to no good and with the flying fist and calls to warn us away they went back to the woods and no violence had come of them but when we knew they were gone and had taken to the woods again it was as if a drum inside the woods was always gently struck in there, a low beating in slow walk down near the roots and knees.

This Miruelo, great navigator of a lost sea, some ocean no man can tell would even exist outside the blown realm of his thistled head, some mapless weed he must dream up and spout off about among a trusted company. Doesn't know where we are. Some thousand mile stretch he might hit if he had a week. So fuck his notions on where. Consult him any longer there is no way to do this.

The always and low beating of a drum out there in the damp trees and I picture this with my companion, we envision what a drum of this people would be like, some hide stretched over a cane ring, tendon looped in and hooked through the smoothen hide and around under the whole basket and adorned with some heathen artifacts all baubled attached or so. The always beating like a heart out there in rest but never gone.

In night we give a story out into the air. Just air that comes out of us. It is not the sea and it is not land or trees of course it is air in the shape of our sound in the shape of tales. We trade stories and but trade at once so one might bank into another.

Another starts: There is no winter where she is from. It is like what we have found here but instead of these pools and mud there is only sand and beyond that a meadow where men built stick houses and she led me to a house one of these stick houses and I could have been led to food or to men with sharpened bones and fast arms or led to a trading room and only what was there in that stick house was a gourd of clear water and a reed mat.

In day it was the will of the governor to go inland and that the ships go along the coast until they arrived at port and on this plan our opinion was requested.

The notary with his lost books all lost to the sea or inside the wind this notary put down my response – the lostness of our pilots and the state of our horses not fit for any use and that our words could not be folded into the ears of who lived on this land nor their words folded into what we could hear and so our ears were blind to what and beyond all this our notion of what this land held was empty of any fact save what we saw in front of us which could be kindly noted as fucked in terms of where to settle us and beyond all this what a mind will not mention even to himself what undressed demon waits in this thatch or blended into the sand we tread and beyond all this our food. But to the commissary he felt all this in reverse and that the port of Pánuco could not be far off as our pilots have advised and could not be missed and the first to arrive should wait there and that to embark with all of us on our ships and all our trunks would be to ask our Lord to bring down upon us His iron heel as He has done already again and before that.

These opinions were noted and because the governor was deciding in the way of the most assembled there I asked that my opinion to do the opposite be quite noted and certified.

The governor called for his men who would travel overland with him to prepare themselves for this trip and then he set me in charge of the ships and to this I refused.

How I saw both each of us as men who went up against a thing, and as such how my body was a piece broken off directly from the sacked ore and set upon this earth to come blasted by all what rains down on average men to halt them, I exist on separate terms as a man of hardships than our governor and to convey this would injure our terms – so as the sun will warm the meat of our bodies the same all of us so the moon ripens only me while they lie dark asleep. Is it found a way to bring this up and still eat the same board?

I refuse and hold fast to refuse the charge of those ships in the face of all our governor's beseeching and I paint to him a picture of my honor as a stack of beams gone to punk which all the men have set to flame and our governor begins to see that I will not sail with the ships but will instead test my body versus all terms of the land here and go alongside him on the overland journey. I tell him it is my sense that the ships and those who travel on land will not meet again in this world. This is all noted in the books and Caravallo is set in charge of the ships.

And so it is I go along with the governor and three hundred men and forty horses and for each man he is given two pounds of hardtack and one half-pound of salt pork and we gather ourselves on land. The ships too are prepared to sail along the coast and Caravallo sees to this and I am thankful that I am not wearing the duty of Caravallo to the ships. Looking out from land the ships are there and they begin to get painted there, as if no longer true ships of wood but in my eyes they are versions of ships perfected, the light upon them and how they sit on the water as things at once a part of our world and also a sketch as an artist might make a thing lay flat on his canvas. Did our Lord command this? My strongest notion tells me these ships will not see our governor again nor he these ships. That our split here will be so for the rest of us. But our Lord will deem correct what fate these ships run into and I can only see from across that distance what our outcomes might be and may all our men on land and those with Caravallo enjoy His protection and course.

These overland days are long for the things we do not come upon. No man. No altered dirt. Just this sanded ground where armadillos and other armored rats do be. The land unmarked by any home of who might live in this place and unmarked by any who at all. The palmetto tree is our only game on this stretch and it is an easy one to corner but takes us all to bring down. We fell them whole and strip off the woven bark and the strings who run up and down and work our way into the core of each trunk and sculpt out for meals the softest inside part of this tree. The rabble we leave behind for each one of these. For more than two weeks this core is our only game and it is what our Lord intended for us and so again we hack down the palmetto and tear apart its outside in order to be a meal to make itself a thing in our hand so our Lord provides for us a feast again and once again.

Then a river is across our way. It is wide and with a current who has a fist and for a day we spend us to get across with all our men and our horses. The water is almost clear, a shallow pool near the shore with a white sand floor tells us about the goodness of the river. A sandbar at the near shore. And then the river becomes a deep river and the water in it moves along with an unbended fist. Our dear horses who along our journey with their noble walk and their strong eye and courage sent to them from a thousand years of courage behind them put up with the halted stumbles of their masters who beat down jungle with long knives and come upon blasted seas and two-fisted rivers and are we all in this as one our Lord? Our day here crossing has at least a different cloud above it, gathering a self inside a piece of shade or setting the next man to hold him to his strong stories and send him to the far shore. We tie together items in a rafted way and send across in batches what we have and on the side of this a man will swim with his body. We mound our all on the far bank and those already over take apart the rafted what and set out the crossed gear on the sandbar in the sun.

As most of us are on the near shore and only few have gone across we can see some Indians have come through the far trees and move over there in a hidden way and move and hide low. Our men on the far shore are not yet aware that these Indians are in the woods behind them. Our language does not carry past the rumbled sound of this river. We throw a small gesture not a large one but that too does not carry to the far shore. They keep on over there to lay out cloth and other items in the sun of the sandbar and spread them there. We keep on our crossing and the news of the hidden Indians goes with the next man to cross the river and during his cross the Indians there become several and it seems now they are more than several but come as a company of many arms and they spread out along the shore for they are many and each goes down to a knee so that who leads them stands tall above them and above his head rides a tall bended plume.

How can it be that a gesture of a hand or how a body becomes more upright and rigid before you and the eyes become stern with an eyebrow at a new posture and a mouth who less widens but draws in so it's told that together we are at odds and soon a hand will raise up against another hand? Men at arms do they come ready in this life for moving a fast arm against another man? So has it been mapped ahead of us our Lord a mapmaker with his scrolls of us spread out above us or beside perhaps this is what the clouds are – charts of us laid out with what we do pictured there and we tread duly on its lines. Or has our walk led us to our present day and each turn or befallment renders us further for the next turn until we come to the far side of the river and through some gauge we devise or through a notion we can tell the Indians gathered there come ready to mix with us against us?

We turn on them. Our hands raise up against them and their hands come up raised and there is the sound of us all in this test and the Lord is in that sound or He is not. We capture five or six of them. They lead us back to their homes where we find an abundance of maize ready for harvest that our Lord has set aside for us and we give thanks. So here we encamp and repair our hunger and our horses rest.

We continue the way of Florida to the supposed Port of Pánuco and we bring with us the five or six we captured and they as our guides go ahead and two of them stay among us and steer us through great fallen trees who lay as tall as one man the tree laid there in its new and final spot a great arm gray and ridged.

For two weeks there is no sign of any others there in the forest and for two weeks we carve out the heart of palm and for two weeks it is only the heart of palm we eat and we thank our Lord for providing these gifts to us and the vigor of our thanks to Him seems among the men to subside each day yet praise to Him is given and I see to it each man brings his full voice and his wide open eyes looking forward and full awake in this rejoicing. Our Lord can hear the timbre of our voices for He can hear our very heartbeats and the voices we must all have inside us who speak with us and bargain withinside us and test our resolve.

We march through this heated woods and two weeks has passed when coming forth to meet us is a native lord and he is carried up above his people on their shoulders and in front of this array like buzzing insects there are small ones who play strange music from a reed flute and these small ones weave among themselves and dart and bound lightly in the undergrowth and hide their heads like the armadillo can do and this lord who flies above his people wears a painted deer hide and teeters there on shoulders and it is this appearance of flying above the ground without any shoulders between him and the sand that he does wish to convey, the natives below him with sticks and leaves and hanging moss tied to them at one with the land about them.

I doubt the shape of this world. Where we find ourselves. As a band of Indians appear to us in these woods with their reeds and with their plume and their sounds all odd to hear so also we appear to them with our leather and our cross-bow and our belts and to them also the sound we carry has no truck with them no weight at all except that it is not a silence there between us so our exchange in these woods is a slim bag of gestures and through this we are both commanded to gauge if we are here in peace or have we come here to be against thee. How has a man come to be the judge of this? The condition of a shape of where we are and I can signal to you our Lord I can refer to where you are for it is I alone who keep these maps of you and keep what you draw for us here upon this sand and soil and I have come to know our lot is drawn and you have sketched with great love the charts of my step revealed to me the moment I step and I have come to know my past and come to know the great distance and I have come to know that here in these woods with only the sound of air and birds and wind and a broken twig and a judgment placed before me what to be with these natives I know your maps of love for us are like great hands who live about us and guard and fend.

We move into the sand between us. In front of the cacique the ones who play odd music part and move off into the side bush and so the cacique comes forward. He is upheld in his lift and then he is down from above and on with us this ground. His arms raise up. His palms upward. From off his arms away falls off his deer hide and his bare arms rise. He comes forward his arms held out he comes alone to come toward us.

In kind our governor walks out ahead of our parted men his slow walk who scolds the time he spends to be ahead. We part us and our governor moves into the sand where this cacique his arms bare and upheld our governor does approach and we are ready when the cacique slowly puts his arms around our governor and lightly holds him with their bodies facing and against. This embrace a greeting or some other it wasn't sure. Our governor seemed slept there and he waited in the silence of us all. Slowly released our governor stood and this cacique held up his palms and arms again and looked into the sun and spoke some brief announce.

This cacique and our governor each spent a piece of time making gestures to the other and it was sketched to this cacique that we were going to Palachen and to the Port of Pánuco there and through the motion of his hands and from his voice it was known to us that he was at odds with the people of Palachen and that he would lead us to Palachen and that his arm and the arm of his people would join in with us to reach Palachen and if there was a spar then these all arms were together in such a spar. The cacique took the painted deerskin he wore and he handed it to our governor and our governor then grandly set out on the ground some bells and beads on a piece of bright cloth and the governor stood as tall as he could stand and with his back like a tree is straight and his jaw set high as he was pleased to show how pleased he was to bestow these beads and metal bells to the cacique who was called Dulchanchellin and who turned and walked into the trees and his people followed him into the trees and we all followed them into the trees toward Palachen.

DULCHANCHELLIN AND PALACHEN

We followed Dulchanchellin and his people and one might have a thought about the faith we handed over as a blind man is led through an unknown hall of rooms and how this faith is more easily handed over when for weeks the heart of palm was only what fed us and our fear of lostness was so great and complete although our lostness was not a spoken thing of us and how a new land to a body causes that same body to believe in the help that is sent for the belief is that there is a goodness ahead and otherwise to otherwise hope is hopeless. How do you follow a man if you are already against yourself? The marching of the sound of us in those trees it is enough to cast away that foe inside us I speak for every man here. It can be no other way.

Inside the trees it became night and we all continued and reached after a time a river who ran with great depth and haste. We heard this river for some leagues before we met this river in our path. There came from off the sides a coolness who drifted up and along the river yard and in that coolness and in the night darkness we constructed a canoe to help us cross the river and even so and even with the help of the men of Dulchanchellin this crossing took us from that night to the next day and next night.

The time has come to reveal the death of Juan Velazquez de Cuellar the impatient, and he was mortally so. And he was mortally courageous some might say of him and did not judge well the current he believed his horse could swim across and Juan Velazquez de Cuellar mortally on his horse they rode together into that river. It was as if we slept there in our feet and a dream became over us for none of the men could speak to warn him away from the river as a voice is unable in a dream so our voices became mute and the sound of the river was what he heard and rode into the water and soon came to overturn and to go along with the current instead of at an angle as a swimmer would have done and Juan Velazquez de Cuellar held the reins of his horse in some try to stay his head into the air but instead the reins pulled the head of his mount down into the river and they both went to the water under and did not come up to live again with us. We stood there in our feet and some men went along the river but there was no sign of him or his horse. In the day the Indians of Dulchanchellin found the horse downstream and told us where we could find Juan Velazquez de Cuellar and near all our men were bent in sorrow for this the first lost of our inland group and that was an unfortune and this man who for his final choice rode himself and one good horse into a current died dead this day. And it was as if our Lord had called down to fetch one of us in trade for some other of our luck. The tables then more even. And in this as well how to walk all of us into the next. The stitch of who was further. The quiet camp we held into the night. The river sound in night and most of us ate of his horse.

Through in these trees for another day and upon the village of Dulchanchellin and there we were not there a full day and we were fired upon, these arrows from the men of this village. Though our Lord decided that none of us would be injured. A small group of us gone into the woods and trees for water and in there the whistle of arrows and by the morning they had all fled and the village was of a quiet a body did not rest inside, a quiet as if at any time it would no longer be so.

On out we went in the morning, fled of that silence or the silence of a fearful people or the quiet of impending unquiet and along the road there came from behind us some Indians prepared for war and they crept low and hid behind giant fallen trees and shot arrows at our rear guards. They wanted nothing of the talk we presented between us. Then our governor set a few of our men hidden along the road in ambush. In time the Indians were surprised and we captured less than five of them. These captured Indians became guides for us through land that was difficult to cross for the swamps and the giant fallen trees it had in it.

I could not know the heart of any man. Such an unknown heap such awful guesses I would extend. But I do know the heart is like water so it bends to fit inside what vessel holds it. The changing shapes of us. I couldn't keep a tally of any one much less. A master of his body at one moment and then within a day enslaved and guiding his captors through his known lands. And death does have a say in this, how when presented with a choice one doesn't walk into her last arms.

And on until Palachen where unnoticed we were in a hide and we were quiet as a man becomes when a hard journey has ended and the journey was more than worse of what it might have been and quiet as if waiting to enter one's own house after long travels so the image of this haven has been rendered as a wish for so long so to savor the view as something near unable to be at all. Quiet in this solemn reverence and the clarity of what one bird sang as we attacked the village of Palachen from horseback and on foot I will not some time soon forget. There were women and the children of these women and so we rode in unchallenged and set to discovering grand stores of maize and we knew the Lord was looking down upon us. And soon the men of Palachen who had been hidden returned and with a strong arm. They had become ready to make war. And so they went about this with great speed and skill and burned the houses where we had set ourselves up inside of in. They gathered their women and their children. One cacique of them we held captive and this brought them to an angry pitch. They returned again and in the days who follow they returned. We consulted with the cacique and he told us of a nine-day journey to Aute where squash and maize and fish from out of the sea were being.

And so Aute became our next to be. The next of a possible next abundant place or resting place or some haven from what we had chosen to march through.

THEM AT SEA

At sea on ships and the men on those ships I try to imagine their spirits and how they carry themselves if they do at all as if some great wind has not carried them off or sent them under or some sea madness come over them for the lostness they inhabit is of the most severe of any lostness a man can live inside or any of the whirlpools unmapped they sail into and spin down into the earth's underground there could be a dozen other of this kind of sea ending who would take our ships into some other aspect but for now I try to imagine our ships as steadfast sails along a steady wave.

TO AUTE

Leaving Palachen for Aute was a true single effort to bring our lives with us. The swamp we crossed the Indians knew of of course and as we all waded waist deep in this and made our way around giant fallen trees the Indians fired upon us and well. For eight days it was a running togetherness as they ducked behind whatever could be there and our minds grew taxed of a burden for thinking they were everywhere and from behind any tree an Indian could become and fire with his skill an arrow well. What a tax it can build a massive unsettle and there is nothing to compare it with in the civil life as there is death to meet you if a step is taken in the wrong and there is death to meet you if for a moment you are not so sharp that you miss a mere shuffle of some canopy and death is there to meet you. Other than an accidental violent to befall you in the civil life there is nothing to place alongside what this tax will do or what a severe ending might happen if. We go with the utmost. A known watcher and his eye upon us.

We place ourselves Our Lord in your protect. We ride our horse into the fast water and when we die those of us who remain invoke the plan you had set out for the dead.

But what kind of prayer was answered when a man dies for his one bad draw?

Although we ate his horse I had a dream come to me regarding Juan Velazquez de Cuellar in a sleep we held in this unplanned grove with sentries posted. At once upon my sleeping he came to me and his mouth was moving but it was the sound of the ocean to come out of him or maybe it was the sound of water and wind and he carried a chime like you might get to see at a station in a far valley. He stopped in front of me with his mouth on. There was a gathering of cover. A green hesitate. And then an actual wind of a kind who has not beset upon us here in this wet land but it was a wind from where we come from.

Our Lord continues on with us and each man his own version of. It is enough of what to know.

The next day from the grove I saw the tracks of man ahead of us and so prepared our ranks by the mention of this. Their ambush came to nothing is what happened to them and to us. Feeling settled in our way as we came against them we doubled back and from both sides on flanks left and right we attacked and took the lives of two of them. Dead Indians of our hand in work. And the only hitch in all this was that my injury was. Aside what had befallen some others in our ranks it was a minor gash from a chop come down, delivered by hand and in the hand a wooden blade is what he had.

You will not be the sole witness our Lord you can not be the sole witness to the wound it is slight why is this wound not more complete for me why is this wound not a drastic shape for to pronounce to these men the sureness of my stance with them. It requires so little but to pay it no care would poison what is beneath it so I wrap a cord of hide around and fasten shut the wound and I know your eye is in there behind that cord I know your eye is many that it can not be counted, your eye inside all our every wound here and there is not a man who would want to be let be.

There is a spell of eight days as such, on an edge for the prospect of an ambush. And then out a league from Aute we are set upon, the rear guard surprised by an Indian group and they were not perceived and so they laid upon our rear guard some great havoc. And of all of our hidalgos to return to assist it was a boy some Castilian and this Avellaneda went back in the direction of this holler and Avellaneda received an arrow which traveled just to the top of his breastplate and passed near entire through his neck so that only a small piece still appeared in front and most of it showed up out back his nape and so the Lord right there came to him this Avellaneda and brought him to the end. I have never put much study on the final words of a man dying so this too was a jumble of places and his people I suppose they must have been and some request to haul forth as if there goes a man here who would complete such an errand my word though I promised to his expiration I would do it. No one of us is heavy any longer and we carried him that league to Aute.

Before the people of Aute had abandoned their homes they set fire to their homes and burned their homes to the ground so that we could not use their homes or so it appeared to us their homes had been burned by an invasion who came before us or so it was hidden how many Indians once lived in the homes of Aute?

On me I resemble an invasion as I go. I move as a moving assembly up in arms against itself and any thing. I will have a moment. A private scout to see. And then I advance with all my inner againstness. I find myself a marvel that I proceed at all though I marvel again at the enormity I carry and at the lands inside me yet to fold out. Not alone we advance into these.

A theater of burned homes we spread into. On guard for the waiting or the hidden bow and we discover the squash and maize on its ready leg and the frijole. And we are nowhere. We rest for two days. Of which an eye is out for the hidden bow and the return of some sharpened stick or the quiet path of an arrow set out by these giant naked men and we are nowhere. This village of Aute where there was some promise of fish and so from that we build our hope to see our ships again the sea must be within a few or near enough god damn for the supposed fish. We rest here for two days to discover we are nowhere. We mend the holes in us and we eat these found abundants over the cooking fires these smaller versions of charred mats left behind like the burned homes. Beyond our hearing and our see there must be a watching some of them. Some band in their naked hide in a state of much about to. High nowhere of the utmost it seems the most nowhere at night, between days as if some unseen number is wiped away and a new number is written on the slate, the increments of our stay, the measure of our sum here added up and set anew with the dawn and the prospect to fill the next day with anything but the same unknown and so we deem our nowhere then impermanent. We do this to move. And so the governor spells our coming tale.

Be of this forewarned. There is an Andrés Dorantes. And seven other horsemen and commissary and fifty soldiers on foot and myself with meat at the behest and order of our governor to leave Aute and go to look for the sea as if it could be missed were it there at all but in our nowhere it was some of us set out for the sea in some beyond of us.

But one of the things of it was the Rio de la Magdalena and that we had already crossed it and knew a piece of it so was ken to us this water led us out to the sea in its winded path. We reached the mouth of a bay and it was true vespers with its oysters there for us in the shallows and the abundant thanks we gave was to our Lord our provider and protector and planter of oysters praise be for the harvest of these unforgiving rockish clams we pry open and finger in.

From this group on the following day twenty set out to find the sea, explore the coves and bays beyond where we were. Most of our group stayed there with the horses near the oyster bed and in the day found shade and some attempted to repair and others could be seen doing elsewise and I for most of that quiet day spoke in close with our Lord so that He might find for us some guidance but that also He might take me aside as He does and He finds a place for me to sequester and in my silence He builds in me the great tower of wooden beams and He commands from the top of this skyward peak to mine ears alone the needed terms the needed hymn of how I find adequate comport. How I carry my body handed down from Him a vessel filled as to the limit with the enormity He sends to me alone. I find my silent apart and I fall into an avail no rustle no commote could enter and it is here He finds me and I am two hands held in front of me cupped and turned Himward and it is poured.

The twenty men returned the following night of that following day and they had only the news that the sea was far and beyond where they did reach and the coves and bays had stretch to them and past an eye to see where. And so with this we return to the governor.

In Aute upon our return to the governor there was an unpleasant to the sight that even in the deep wretched state we found ourselves upon our return to the governor it was impossible to not find the shock in one's self and to once again have surprise at how profoundly tested we were by the odd land in where we found ourselves and by the chapters our Lord had devised for our love and our benefit and how to believe it was so was even still in itself another test in war to have to host within. For not only had a wild sickness laid down its fever blanket upon the men entire but also as the men did battle with this sickness that brought them weak and beyond all rational sense and they crawled inside their own bodies and fever visited down upon their limpnesses and they wasted it was then they were set upon in night by Indians who came with a flying wrecking and brought our men dear close to the final draft and even killed a horse. It was near unable for the governor to recount. The men had even some of them in their craze become wary of a branch or leaf or bird who moved. It was a going from dire to more so. Repair seemed like an unable.

It was decided to undo our camp and move for to move has been our only path our only way toward some other-where some place we were not. The picking up and break-ing camp if camp could be what it was at all and after grim assess we moved as a plodden wrack. An assembly now of the moaned and wailing and together we left Aute and set in the course of where our scouting group had discovered oysters and in our state of driven down we march and our Lord carries some of us more than others. It can not be painted another way. Nor can it be retold in any manner who can properly hand over how difficult in the most abun-dant ways this was. There were not horses enough to carry our sick and we had no remedy for the sick or even some remote hint at what could better them who languished. Hard to recall as well in this was the state of our horses who also were drawn and wasted entire in their walking sleep. How our Lord has given them a courage and stillness and nobility my heart comes up against itself when I recall them in the woods there. But we plodded and the weight of our travel in this way I had a weight on myself about it. I had pictured the oyster beds as a possible replenish and some shade as that was where we had just done this eating. But also there was the sea, although we didn't find it, only that it was beyond where our where. How a decision is made I can only recount a band of men who were near their lastness. I can not put it here another way. Our Lord as witness saw us there beneath the canopy as wrecked men who required of the life a man leads at least a semblant afternoon. We hadn't had an afternoon in weeks. But decisions make a man I have known. So we are made. And we plod us to the oyster beds.

Our ruined horses I apologize to our Lord for their ruin I can see them taut thin and draggled as a coat becomes in rain I can see them as our Lord sees them in rows of thin dark walkers enburdened with the sick who flop and tumble on them moving with their troubled grace their unhealth a matter of form I see them down through the tops of trees as we go I am in communion I can see our ruined horses and I ask forgiveness of the utmost as I have not before.

How done we found ourselves. So gone was our state and hope it is now unable of any recall what we could tell ourselves why we found ourselves there and we could not tell ourselves how to leave it it was a special home we made for ourselves a new home inside this charred hollow. This bind. To be in a place it seemed unable to be in. And as well to be in this same place and have no exit from it.

But faith in our Lord God as he stands beside me is the most curing of a man I can not tell enough how this is so. And for good as the time had drawn up to us all when the horsemen in their private den conspired to abandon and go off to some unknown but without us all instead just them on horses would go. And although the truth of this spread as quick there was only sickness that our governor could do then, overrun by illness his weak admonish was less than much. He could do nothing against it. And since the breed of these horsemen was of the hidalgo and other blooded ilk they would not head their way without first a notice to our governor. So this intention was brought forward and we all astounded the horsemen with a reduction of their plan, and questioned their role on an earth where they would leave to die underneath the shade of some odd plants the very men who have gone armed with them to now and could a man do such a thing and if on the far side by chance they reach some otherwhere is the sun who rises there and the wind is it all enjoyed as if this way of Florida never was? With all this they abandoned their plan and to this day I still am unsure where they might have gone that would have tossed them any different coin for unless they had been guided by a dream who showed them a route unknown to the day there was no figured way to go but back and in that way there was nothing for them but a chain of misery run in reverse.

I come to know that when it is dire and then beyond there gets less a notion of caste or rank or what you have learned or who has sewn your leather.

Until then there had not been a council but now the governor calls a council by each a man will come to him and tell some idea of how to go. There is always to go. Each man approaches and each man comes to some plan that when I hear of it I can only think of us as a gone assembly, each man either too damned of his body to utter any sense or some of us able in a way but not in the habit of arriving at anything more than who to fall in behind and then a lucid few go ramble now they have his ear they ramble on some vision they had or they ramble on that notion of return and one of us is certain we need boats for us to sail on but any tool or hand or device physical and otherwise does not exist for us and a sled to pull our sick is proposed and a return to the squash is added to all this. Our governor in such council with each man does note the very plan brought forth and I among the canopy strike through an unseen rule of them all. The notary now another man with his mouth open and his body on the ground and his eyes are there with him.

From out of this council it should be noted that our decided and agreed upon way to go should indicate our wits and also how gone deeply in reserve our stores of us had become, because it was decided we could sail from there. The ships not having been built or conceived or at hand at all possible but yes we decided to sail. In boats. As I have told here.

Our Lord God as He sees a proper coat to put on us we have gathered to be guided by you.

But it would be taller to list what we did not have for building ships than to list what we did have.

The outlandishness of it caused us all to need a rest and to seek quiet so to let the plan smolder and to think about our no rope and our no pitch or oakum and our no tools and our no iron or forge and our no idea of how to go about any of it as one who knows how to build a ship and so we rested to further ponder and so that God our Lord might while entrusted so direct a man to where he might best serve.

I could not sleep for our lack had mustered in me the want to find a way from our maze of unhaving – there must be a thread we could follow back to reason to any knowable turn of where we were to tread out our next our way away but I ran into the endless boxes of ends as a hallway bends into its final hem and you come left up against a wall who gives you no further room for the end of any hall ends up as a door into some other or it will end up an ending you hadn't foretold yourself inside you there was no waying known and then you slow it all into the quiet sense of what you have just come up against and that an ended hallway is what only can be a turning of it and of you and so you turn for that is what only you can do is turn back and trace again where it is the from of you and so you go back and your own thread is the one thread you can follow back to where there was a corner you could recall who had a hope of some anything but I return proud to the cause of us by word I return and cast myself down that unwent hallway and cast my chance down my Lord I cast myself into the hollow mold and I cast myself into what can only be the single hallway you set for me is this the only hallway you have set for me for it is mazy and it ends abrupt and does not continue and ends it so all might end as such and how I could not sleep you can see how I couldn't sleep.

And so only the seconds of us pass as we ourselves pass into the nexted moment. The pure of us. The step of what's coming. And what that is is is. Our only.

Unslept and so I rise but none the closer to an open door.

And from the nowhere comes a man who from our company has a claim to know how to make bellows from deerskin and from a hollow tree and God ordained this for God had selected from the company this man to speak.

Bearing over to the stillness. Let us allow us not this pausing. This quiet and a slowing down of the walk we were on. Measure all this pause and then an ellipsis. An opening written down as if to breathe into the live a gap. Take a moment in this I solicit, us entangled in a momentous. Breathe along with all of them there in the solemn and only shaded den they win.

Here is the golden piece of the consensus – after the consideration of all we had not, in supply and in thought and in general wherewithal, we then decided to further entertain this notion. How could that even cause what I just mentioned? That is the golden piece of a man so stranded and against an element.

After the bellows was proposed and put us all in favor of the boats it was then laid out how in the course of some unknown span we'd get some boats together and in this outlaying it was decided a fixed number of incursions back to Aute would have to be and that every third day we kill a horse. To feed ourselves. In order to be men alive.

God ordained this and yet the underwriting of it I'm incapable to know. There is always the want to know the structure of His command but as we end up each day with another day lined up ahead I come to find any notion of His trend is without note and has no seen outline and is lost entire if I'm grasping at it.

And if we left on boats there was no plan to return is what is of the utmost here. There was the sea with boats we come to make and our stores well planned to expire and all our metal melted down and us a group of men on four boats cast off into the next and once set as such there is no returning.

WE BUILDED BOATS AND DIED

Our one carpenter began the building of the rafts who had no hull but instead a flattish deck. For putting together rafts we gathered together all our metal from stirrups and spurs and crossbows and whatever else we had in iron and this was melted down and it was melted with the bellows made of horsehide, the alchemist with his methods so they need the horse to play magic with this iron wreck and in doing so remove from the very horses they require the pieces which amount to their value to us, now removed and the horse can stand and wait to be ended for us and become our food of all things. An alchemist is only so much. And from the bellows melted iron comes the tools, saws and axes, nails. We pour the melted iron into a sand mold with clay and with the seldom rocks about us we file upon the stone these nails and sharpen axe blades. The caulk in between the wood who makes up our decks in between to fill in where varied lines abut the caulk is of the oakum from palmettos. The pitch entire, in a slather among the undersides, was a mixture that Don Teodoro the Greek had devised and it was brought out of the pine tree by the way he had known and his father had known.

While in construct we made incursions back to Aute to gather what we could and along these ways there were skirmishes with the Indians and they put a cut into the numbers and our skin we have.

Our men, they set out into the inlets to accume the shellfish and into the coves who were near. I try to feel what our men felt out there so near to our encampment they were by the cove into the water of the cove. The sharp oyster beds cut into the feet and to move in the water is a slowness. There is a quiet around you there. The sun is almost welcome. Is almost a wanted sun up above the window of the sea you wade through the bending sights below all bended and rippled you pass a hand through that waterpane and see your arm take an angle to the oyster there. If all is well there will be a sound of how you pass a hand into the neath. Unlike any other sound, there are certain sounds only our own hand can make. And so it jingles a bellish chime. Or what I can not hope to describe but you must believe in the silence the note is beauty the note is clear to me. Those men so close to our encampment there on a stillness day the silent arrows in paths to them from the hidden groves, the skill and brute with which they. I have a heart who lives with them. In heavy lode it goes with them to the seabed where they drifted off from. The Indians in the hidden groves an eye on the man of whom, an arrow gone out from the single hope, and skill aided that flight into the flesh of us, the neck and breast of us, the gut and out the far side, put through with these arrows so final my loden heart becomes with them and falls among them there so close. I try to be among them. They fall, a quickly set upon few and these Indians retreat in a silented go to the back from where.

Our waterskins are made from horses. The meat we dine is horses. We are carried here on horses and our horses continue steady if at all able. I have at least one confession. As all the horses die for us I have not once taken flesh of them for me. I could not. So beyond what I could do even as our sins have placed us here in a premise beyond all fathom I still could not find myself past the reach of what I know of all our horses. To become partaken of them. I could not join in to this. I have a confession of this and I did not bring in to me the flesh of any of our horses. Our waterskins are made from horses. And it is all I can to lift one against the dryness. We all succumb at a point but at what? I don't go beyond our horses.

Forty more of our men die of sickness here in our boat-building.

The last horse was eaten. The boats on the eve of done.

The merits of our sins put us in such a place as to make it near shut of any rock to use for ballast it was deep work to find a stone for us to use. Such was the land in where our sins had put us.

We left there on five boats and on each boat was about fifty men and our boats all laid down into the sea so that only a piece of each deck was above the water. And again to call what we set out on boats is to praise too well these flat decks banded and caulked. Just us all rafted is what to call it. Some oars from savins were in a side ladle and famished we all drifted out into the bay with our waterskins and with our need to travel from there and we departed from what we called the Bay of Horses and set out in our away.

The water we drifted on was only waist deep and we used an oar against the stillness to get us through the inlets what became no sea but instead the shallows we found ourselves in. How far for certain would our misdeeds or the hills of our sins captured in hills of misdeeds how far could it swim with us and let us come up against another inlet another false aperture another cheating gap who began to look like open ocean but instead as a mountain trail would give itself to a peak who when upon it becomes a false summit and the leveling gives itself to even more trail and even upward so the most untrue inlets and gaps appeared and happened to us and as quickly as a heart can lift at the hope of it as quickly sunk it'll.

The inlets having run out for us after seven days there was an island near the shore. The raft in my charge went ahead and from the island five canoes approached us and they had seen us and so they left their canoes and entered the water with their bodies and they allowed their empty canoes to drift toward us although it was hard to say how empty they could be there is nothing that could not be a danger there is nothing so clearly one way and not some other way. These drifted hulls as quiet as the days leading up to them but drifted hulls as such do speak we all heard. The other rafts went ahead and to the island. And as if it was ours on that island the mullet and dried roe were taken up and with us for the necessary of it from the few houses there.

Past the strait who makes itself between the mainland and that island we furthered and came to a shore of where. The canoes who drifted to us were towed with us now and now ashore we used these canoes under the decks of our rafts to float us and this lifted our decks and we were lifted also with the hope this brought us to.

Following the coast in the direction of what must be then the Rio de Palmas. Our waterskins so dearly knotted dearly provided to us the skin began to rot and with them our fresh water was something gone and so again we became to that place where our sins would put us in hunger and in thirst and without good charts in us to know well the line we aught. The hunger became our note to sing. Hit over and again as if in no way could any judge of us see to it that we come upon another store of dried fish and it was a hunger days long drifted there, inlets invited and became shallow and a harm and through all these and days of this we drifted and drank no water nor we found any. No root. No roe.

Now come days and nights of a drifted way. The slow creaking of our decks and there is a moon who lights us in night and who puts a trail of moonlight on the vastness of the sea between us and the moon it lays a path to she. Behind us the events are stacken like felled oaks laid down in rows the land behind us as a referent only and a breeze acrosses us in night as if some colder land existed so to tempt us to forget the present land the present sea as all about us as is possible. The sea now between us and land a stretch so reached to look back to where was poor hope and between the land and us was builded an uncountable map of sea volumes. Our nights were slept as much as a crouched mass of us could retire to it, our nights were dark nights on the sea calling shouting to the other boats for our closenesses on the sea who tented us in the canopy of stars who bended from one shore to the other in all directions and a single star was for any of the men some point beyond our what that could not be reached but only seen from far away the cranking shelf turning all night of stars one next another the rotated roof above us the pinholes in linen draped above us the white fires in back of it all lighting the dotted sky in even and in odd lights and us below it all a huddled audience unclean and so adjacent to the next a packed assembly I see few of us looking upward in night to reckon our place among them or to reckon how many more nights we might come to be at all among them let us not soften this recall.

I sit us rafted there in nights. It is an almost quiet if there is one. The bad nourish of the men keeps us in a solemn. The groaning of the men. The sea closest to our decks it washes in a sound against the sides and we drift at night. Our bodies uncloaked against the weather even though uncoated is what we'd be either way. One of the men hutched in nearby is drawn and little remains of him and I wait here our Lord I wait here for the turn of his eye for the moment his head might lift and I know our Lord I know there is no return and I know there is no thing toward of which all of us sail. How there can be it can't. In night we capture ourselves inside us and go visit those ensaddened rooms where the moments so darkly drawn and brought back again with new light and new edges like a hand who disturbs the tapestry inside the fresco so this visit repaints a life already been, untrusted and believed at once for the visit is what he calls the visit alone is the matter. His eye bended down in such a visit. His room a stolen room spent down on matted grass with her that dear inside neck the loosened collar and a shoulder how it lights itself and puts a crest above the grass the lavender was her design in hemp oil and in rose, the fallen what we wear coming to its mounded fall the matted well in which, the bended inness of a waist and on its edge inside the light who comes down from noon there is a faint silken hair like blown grain but as fragile and minute as the near lost edge of wool. The light a criminal beside the eye together build-ing this ungone forever bit, lasted from then on and visited again as a moment as a guide back to the moment and from there depart and brightly sing in the gaps. His room a stolen room tethered unkindly to the where in which we find ourselves. I wait here for his eye and I wait with him so his eye can remain and solely visit back into what all remains as it would seem the upcoming has only to arrive to tell what we might already divine.

71

PAST INLETS AND TO THE SEA

We are among the sea now. There is no tempering its darkness. In the day we scan out for some notion of land but no
piece of it appears to us. I am in charge of men here on this
boat this raft these men all brook no hedge they come down
with us as one gang floats here on the sea of our Lord He
has cast us here as if our sins could add up to some place as
we are some place so dire and so bright the sun come down
on us is how bright how the sea is black still and how the
wood we tied and nailed is held in a creak as a sea wave lifts
us and drops us and the far boats the far rafts come and go
from sight like sides of a flag in wind or the fig in back of its
white leaf or how an eye of the horse you ride is hidden but
then turns to show you the great eye who sees more than I
could soon guess. Bestow us from here I could ask of any
horse but we have had them all and would they not come
included in our sins? Our deep sins who delivered us here
so we can hide among each other with ourselves only to
counsel, here to hide our notions of the sea and our damn
boats against it, our water gone, hidden is our sense of end
and how it will visit down upon us. Very smote by the air
we take in.

Here and there an order goes out. Here and there a man takes it upon himself to put an oar into the sea and try to guess some thing. To in a way vote one way or another on how we go. There was a try at first to remain near shore to see it there but wind and current soon brought us away from that.

There was a night. I can not say who slept there were fifty-one men on my boat I could not know who slept and who did not but there was a night it was still and it seemed as though the men slept around me. The moon was with us. And I turned my body. We were in general a splay, some back to back, some rested back on the knees of him in back of him. So I turned my body. I was not leaned for myself and the inspector as men in charge we could not lean on another man so truly. As such, self supported, I turned my body to an angle of the moon as a man would to converse with another. There was a new side awake in me as the men slept around me. My back was straight and I felt as if I had just taken a full draught of water and a cooler wind was directed into my breathing. My eyes became open and I could almost stand. To recall this now is a double knife at once in service and then also turned inward. For the manner I held and for the shape the men were in. I turned my body in the direction it only could go. Drawn as I was to the way I went. There was no other way. I revisit this in full and clear sight. My body at the angle of receive, the angle of counsel and the angle of to share between us some nugget dug up and we both are glad for it in our grins and eyes. It is here with my body turned that I atoned for sins but also cast them aside. My sins have got me here and so I left them here in night when awake among them all I turned my body and sent them all downward and aside. I could know this. I know my sins and who other would acquaint as much? This is what I mention. This was in night.

There wasn't a way then in night with my body turned to lug any longer those sins who got us all here for here was about as ended as a man could spend so those sins must have done their share and could do no more to guide us any worse to send us off into sea without provision without how to sail or steer could there be any stronger fell than what became of us for our sins could it now be they've run out of shit for us and done I cast them aside. They're all slept it's our sins I manage alone I cast them alone. I've casted alone these what all of us have lugged. Turned me to receive and to claim and a double knife it is to recall.

These sailing days we come lost in what could be. All horizons a constant hoax.

These sailing days into nights. When a burned quiet spread out around us. Our reference dwindling down to what we heard, the other boats at times. This was the most alone these fifty-one men could come to. Our land shrunk down to a little dome around us floated there as away from what we know as into that unmapped whited map the stars above us rude guides for men unacquainted with their old assistance.

Our water is near through. I guess at what I might command
if one of us passes here. Do we just him overboard?

A sea madness settles into few men but in whom it sits I wish nothing more else than it. The steady back and forth. The wish to not infect the other men but with a rock so large in one's throat it's not able to not touch another man with that unsettle. It could begin with a slow sense of far away and how the eye is cast out beyond all seeing. A sense a man is not a part of us, he's gone his way and is headed off, a cracked veteran awobble, unsteered into his other next. Gives himself a pact and law dependent on no other man. This volunteering into the woods of the sea. How could a near man not land even some of this? Even just to post witness to such a leaving calls to mind that such a thing is possible at all.

It is odd that the men who wail in open but just once a loud and from deep within wailing I commend them and see them safe from the madness. In the bellows is his good statement and then it is gone and what returns is the world at hand. Christ if we could all once do this casting what sure stead we'd gain.

It is either way in madness or as a man released of what he lugs that we head into this unlighted chart and none of it would seem to weight itself down with much grace upon us. It is never far off what dire minutes we live.

There are the timbers who raft us and to check up on how the caulking holds. There is the manner in which the timbers are assembled. We have toes of which a man could stare and mend, the terrible grooming away of what's upcoming.

And night comes upon us every night. The false quiet and the stars who hand out their false guides or is it us the false readers of their olden signs? But it's night when our shelters come up around us and we cove inside to that slept oaken room.

WE COME UPON THEM AND THEM US

Thirty days in such a float, our water now exhausted our food nearly gone. And in night it was noticed a canoe came in a drift to us. This was a real canoe as there were many false ones we noticed in those thirty days but in night this was an actual. We called out but it did not arrive and instead it drifted off again and in the night we did not follow.

In the dawn there was a small island we landed on to see if fresh water could be there but there was none. And anchored there a storm came up and laid a hand down on us with such hands that we could not leave and so we laid there in six days of wildness and rain and a wind who was always.

The men took sea into themselves for the thirst they had not known before. Six days of without and some men did not caution themselves and took more sea than should be and came to die there on that island as men who from Spain would end there. Five men died this way from the sea inside them and do you need to know much more about this island? Is there some piece your self can not imagine? The hardship we dwelled in can not be limned in adequate phrases and you must bring with you the sketch of us and know it was more unchosen. There was no hope in many and little hope some had it was us in an ended hall.

This low hope sent us off into the sea although the storm it kept its way and did not abate there was again no other way to be and so we sent us off and God our Lord was our guidance we entrusted ourselves to Him for in the time as it was there was only to entrust and to lay oneself over to the care of Him. In the sea our boats were logged and near sunken. We were moved in ways that meant us to no longer live alive. Our side canoes had come undone and went away. We pointed us in the direction from where the canoe had come but soon we were so blown aside as to have no bearing and the water coming up over our boatsides was enough to snuff out any thoughts of living this life. We lived as though death was sure. But as God who then was pleased to bestow His favor in the time of greatest need for it was as such we came into a dusk and in there we rounded a point where land came out into the sea at an unlikely purpose and on the far side of this point there was great quiet and refuge and the blasting had traded in for quiet on the lee.

Canoes came out to meet us and we heard them as they spoke to us in their language and then they turned their canoes and went back to where they came from. It was noticed that they did not carry with them any weapon of war or any weapon with them at all and they were large people and their person was well suited for the physical. And so we drifted in this calmness in follow to their houses, which were near the edge of the water. And there we went ashore.

But private it's kept and we'll not forget what we all to ourselves we might have thought our last words in this life would have been. Near drowned, the boats our rafts up against the sea doing unwell at best the sea in a rise about us, tossed entirely, there was not a man I could swear to this who did not mutter what he thought to believe was his last issue here. How our last word has become a noted thing. As if to almost unburden that moment of its weight. For to realize the weight we at the same time blot out the weight by the sight of it. As holding a thing will end the want of it, so realizing the end and that a man's word could be that final one, that holding does also strip away the pure baldness of it. But from a throat unable to get left behind comes that final mutter and could that be anything but not pure? Some quick note to kin or the building of something grander as if he's sending himself off into the next act and no one but his self is there to post witness. Or a hesitating bumble of something dripped out in time just in time to get it down so as to not send off without it being said no matter how ill the line. How worn or laid out. How alike to the repeated waves who bash us into that good next, how alike to the one before.

We went ashore there. The sickest of the men stayed on the beach and laid there in all attitudes and they were like wooden men put together from bended sticks. The governor and I and a few of the weller men went to their houses and there we came upon vessels of water and enough cooked fish for many and the cacique offered these things to us. We took them to the house of the cacique where he and the governor went inside and we all went inside and in there we ate fish. We had with us the maize that we had brought and we offered this to the Indians and they ate it in front of us and asked us for more maize and we gave more maize to them. We also gave to them small metal bells and trinkets which on the rafts had no value but here were items held up by light fingers to test the shine or the note when a bell was shook.

In night we rested in the house of the cacique and slept deeply until in the night we came alive with their attack on us. They moved in quickly with stones and clubs. Not one of us got from the house without good harm done and the governor had been harmed in the face with a hand-held stone. They also descended to the beach where most of our men slept and many lay in dire stead and they attacked us there where much harm was done to us and they did push one of our rafts into the sea where it was taken by the sea and our men died there on that beach where no map has been drawn of it but we had been there and our lives were there with us. We put the governor on a raft and the most wounded also on the rafts as about fifty of us stayed on shore to wage. They attacked three times that night with their brutal and their skill they caused us to retreat each time. I was harmed on the head and not one of us was able to remain unharmed.

Amizol. Raul Vazquez. Elandro y Cuentros.

Some remained interred as souls sacred and at once left there.

Into a color of blue and earth-color, the sea tan and pale. There was enough behind us and I looked back upon it and then it was night and we did not know then it was the first of three nights it could have been the first of any but the night came and lowered us within it. There is a sound of this night darkness. And in it I beheld olden acts.

My olden acts please forgive the cursive of it. The swirled outsideness of this all. So let us all then settle into the below-ground and imagine only where our words can take us. To the recollections inside us. Bended and off to the side. At best if we have some luck it falls into some place.

Floated there in the night and around us only a water map and the waves sculpt us up and down and then up again.

Three days in sea us all rafted close and thirst for the lack of water was of the utmost for there was not any water we could drink with us and our unknown drift brought us to where all sea around us it seemed water we could drink was far off and to cause a man inside himself to not think about water he could drink was the order of our day what we came to want the highest was to not want. And so these side journeys into side tales. A man would offer up a door and we'd go through it. How best to dry one's grass he cut. Who best in Cadiz could fit a saddle, who best in Cadiz for boots. And no man is unheard we have enormous time it is almost rue when a man stops to let another bend in. But it is also then when I set off into my own scrolls and conjure for my own elsewhere a stage whereupon all who come dear to me they stand here and in what act I do not know but they are presented here on this stage in me it is clear who all they are. It seems almost a reverse of what. As if they would be seated and I standed there on the stage for them all to behave upon what I find myself in. But instead they are standed and I can view them all there, shifting weight and held for what cue I have no understanding of. Hours I spend in view from one to the next eyes, a countenance or side glance I wonder what upon. The faces of them all. The several tallnesses.

Onto the water there for three days. Entering an estuary in wild travel we sailed in a weave only our Lord could draw some likely path of an estuary into which we entered and approaching us was an Indian canoe with Indians inside of it and we called to them as we must have had to.

This I recall as us calling out to Indians and as they must have seen us as men also, men of a world as they were men and not birds or water beast so they bore witness to our request as men in need dire need they witnessed our arms in a call to them, we reduced it I believe to the smallest gather between a man, one who is well and one in need and we called as the one not well in arms unarranged and arms upheld and our voice was plaintive at the least if I had exact words to go with how we sounded and had our hands I'd exact upon you this perfect way but instead I can tell you it was this they saw the Indians saw us dissembled there and needy so they coasted up to us. The governor's raft was the first they came upon and the governor requested water for drinking. But a trade was demanded to provide the vessel to carry water and we had no vessel ours all rotted from the days they lived already.

But my heart is split already in the knowing of what is upcoming. I'm almost convinced to convince you some other thing was true. I put to myself the task of telling you.

Don Teodoro who was a man among us demanded that he go with them. The Indians wanting a vessel and for some day born Don Teodoro had himself to go with the Indians back to them and he brought with him a black man un negro de Jesús our Lord I cast myself up to the lights you star down upon us to know as you do the why of this. The insistence of the moment is unable to convey, the moment itself. The falling away of commands the dishevel and dire we lived in stripped away the orders and the chain they all fell into. And they went. Unrafted from us. To them in canoes. And it was solely because he wished to go that we could not stop him and so he went with them and my heart is a beast of itself to recall this departure this separation from us as the living into what he became which was a notion former, an after man. Don Teodoro and his recipe for the pitch we used to seal the boats against the sea drawn out from certain pine trees he knew, Don Teodoro himself casted by himself into the arms of the Indians there.

As if such a trade can be made at all as if the barter was somehow law to whom upon scrolls can read some witness of this honor we receive two of their Indians as hostages and they remain with us in a silence they keep with us. Separated far enough to not hear the other.

In the evening their canoes approach us and the vessels are there in the canoes. And the vessels handed over to our boats are light for the air inside them and no water was inside them and Don Teodoro was not there in a canoe at all and the black man Don Teodoro brought with him was not there in a canoe. In a strange bark thrown at them by their own men from canoes the hostages with us were told to throw themselves into the sea and they tried to do so but some little strength remained in us and we kept them from getting off the boats. There was some waving in anger and a raised arm and cries of anger as the canoes went to retreat and then off back to whence. This leaving had our hearts in a mixture. From out us bellowed a soft sorrow for the sadness and the questions we became to have about why this was just and for the wonderment at what might come next about the Indians.

The morning came, us still rafted afloat there with the sun in its low way rising so to add the vision to what we had been hearing. The sounds of the sea who butts up against and the unplanned groan of a man who has hunger deep in him or some brief fit who has a body call out in response to what could be any olden idea wandered in from ago. The sun lets us see these sounds in dawn it lets us see the clouds and the path of them it lets us see the tips of the sea waves and the way they bend it lets us see the many canoes coming to us from the Indian place the many more than what came to us the last day and in this morning the canoes are many and they are asking for the two Indians who are hostage on our rafts with us to which our governor demands the return of our Don Teodoro and the black man Don Teodoro took with him as if again this barter was something among men.

Among the Indians in these canoes were several lords of their people who carried their own bodies in a way more posed and dour as if around them a piece of honor had been held and they felt in need to revere the solemn mote about them. Cloaks of sable skins were built with leather ties in an odd try which made them beautiful and not of any near thing we knew these cloaks upon the lords and their longer hair let fallen in a manner that I took to be the way in which the heathen comes to believe in fates much aligned in the crude faith they lug about with them as if the hair would tell an early story of how a rock is split to make an infant or the role of the moon in where to find a root to dig up. They asked that we would go with them and that they would bring us to Don Teodoro and to full vessels of water and pleading as such with us in the same event more several canoes crept out and to our sides and began to flank us. We pulled us back and out farther to the mouth of the estuary before we could be closed in by them and out to sea.

They followed out of the estuary and with their canoes they rounded us at sea and became around us for the morning and past the top of the sun's downward upon us. We would not return to them the two Indians we had and so began their war pantomime, an arm drawn back upon a bow that was not there or the lob of a spear that did not exist but an actual rock did happen to us. This fake assault lasted until when the wind rose and the Indians turned back from to where they were.

We sailed until a vespers hour. Instead of Don Teodoro and el negro he took with him there was no man and no man. We commanded us to go. And then it was my raft in front of our other rafts when a point of land was seen and on the far side of this point was a river of a size we had not seen to then.

My prayer for us our Lord I bring to you a prayer for the river we have come upon the color of whom is still I pray the sign of the freshet so needed dearly our men rafted our men dried here in our choice or in the place we can be set for how tall our sins weigh count the measure of them and place us here a point of land some leaf of hope for water some leaf of hope for the lee side of any earthen hedge to fall behind, out of the weather for a rest we haven't known. A lifting of us.

The point of land it did to us an ask and we did tie up there to wait for the other rafts to come. But the governor and his ruined face would not come and tie up there I can not put to you a guess to this indeed the Lord could move a man in such a way as to veer from what a man should do is this not the very split we find among us how we sand down our own best oath to somehow suit the path a man could wish for himself? The split a riven mass who holds the truth one very sided way and then upon the other mass a lifted fist who claims the very else.

There was another bay and the governor landed his raft there and it was there we came together. The great river entered into the sea there and we drank the river water and cooked the maize we had still we went to gather wood but there was no wood on the land here there were no trees but across the river on an island there were trees and it was agreed we would go to the river and cross it so to get the wood we knew would be there.

We set off us in our raft into the river and against all guesses as to how good the current was we were carried with the current and the north wind that our Lord sent down to face our try and with no arm enough of us to help us we were put out to sea.

There is a beyond madness I believe we have in us. A deep yellow like a metal stone who turns and as an ember it heats with the wind up against it. The madness lugged in and out of the rooms of us through doors of us we hide it from the wind the lightest duff which up against the madness it fans the ember into that hottest stone who puts a body along some odd path and writes a script for each man differently and strange this hottest babel is unheard the notions peculiar to each man come alive and now freed enact a rite wholly fucked and bright to only that man and none other. This solitary trip at once outside the man and truly within. A beyond madness who somehow does not ride with us floated here aloud but instead the madness though fanned I do not know how it remains inside these men. It seems for some the lightest alter can throw him into the gut of it. It could be that our hunger has a taller role or the water we have needed and without these deep wants it would avail the stone to become odd within us. But instead we ride floated here and our madness is small for now though I can not believe for good.

Blown out by the north wind and by the current our Lord builded into the great river we took a sounding and we had become into the deep water. And here we drifted out and for two days we sailed and reached us for land in dire throws. What little left our arms could do was not such to land us not such at all to even tell that we'd edged us any more near. My orders to row became almost to me an outlandish. And then a night comes to us there rafted the second night after our river our great river brought itself as a freshet of the Lord into our thirst of it. In night who nears a day we saw there on what should be the shore far off we see the lights of woodfires as small dots on land. We took a sounding and it was three fathoms down so near to shore we came. The smoke of the woodfires on the shore in threads up to the clouds like string from cloud hands fingered to the wooden manikin who in night we chose to not go up to.

It was Don Teodoro we thought of in our choose to not go near the shore in night. For the sun even before it rises will limn the earth a touch enough to guess about it. And the sun did limn enough for us as the earth was brought to us in morning it was clear the other rafts were beyond seeing and they had drifted either severally or alone each far away and we had become apart. Our certain raft alone from the next. What could be more? Then. We took a sounding and the sounding was thirty fathoms and it was not until the dusk had put its early blanket on the day when two rafts came into this view and the first raft we came upon was of the governor.

Do the oceans and seas have a drift or does the ocean have a say in where a barque'll send itself you've come up with streams warm water gone up a coast to carry men back to where yet our coasted way is a piece of chance is it only what a man is up to then willing to endure or willing to give to them I pray our Lord for a vein of hope into which I'll dig in endless pick-heaves axing into the crust of what you send to us in each day what you send to us alone and us alone I see you there as if at all you see me here it is I who command us it is I who guide the men who cut straps to fill their wage. Suss me a better gauge.

It could be said that I told the governor we should catch up the other raft and then as three boats again we could allow our Lord to determine our path as He so truly has done to now. The unbelieve of it our path to now I put that to whom. Our Lord our mapmaker our He who mounds clay into the map we live.

Then our governor did head for shore. He said the far boat was so far as to be unreachable and that he would go to shore instead of to join us all together in three boats as one. Only by the will of each arm can land be had I hear him say as if that vine of sound was a written tome kept safe after all this what we'd. So to the shore he and his men headed and aided by the advice of another captain who was with him on his boat they turned toward the land his will unassailable. We on our boat put down into the sea an arm and then an oar to follow him to land to get us in some way set one way and not another. But for the life and days I walk I thought of our farther boat who out beyond and I can only think their hope was rested on the return of one of the boats to them and here we are in dire row away from them and to the land they have become so distant from. They are the men unlike all other men for the path they have become upon us all a band enbanded to this.

How to say when hunger dulls a man's recollect and dulls his way to see or his way to know and the now is smalled down to what direction might gain us a day of life what way to point a boat so that we do not end our days here on this earth out floated without food and a bored sun leans down as he leans on everything upon our end our chosen end?

We tried to follow the raft of the governor but our done arms could not keep up. He had the strongest men and in a day of rowing it was drawn for us that we'd not keep up with them to land. Seeing this I called out to the governor and said for us to join so that we all had a chance to reach the land but he said back that they as a band alone would have to expend too much to reach land that night. Not least as well was that it was an order and to follow them to land was the order given for us to fall into. I put this to our governor to know from him how we should then follow the orders given our lean hope to reach land.

He said back that it was no longer time for one man to command another.

He said back that it was the duty now as we had come to it that to preserve life one had to do what one thought best and that he would do that to preserve just that and in saying this he turned away with him his raft toward the land.

Knowing we could not follow I turned our raft toward the one at sea and this was our new route and what we did. In drift for a day with the other raft a guess away.

Across the blue and mostly sandcolored sea with the tips of waves the color of sand and not white or blue but instead the color is the color of the sand across this dune in sea and there is not a thing and then of a sudden there is a thing and it is the other raft who waits there in the map of the sea and there on this raft is Peñalosa and Tellez can you in the reachest of your deep heart get to gather what this means to a heart in sea drifted on the look for any Christian who sails any one raft you know is there?

We go to them in the open sea. At a length we attach to them and Peñalosa and Tellez to us. So floated and enjoined enough slack to crest a wave between us we floated. There was a hope to spot the governor and his raft but that was a wish cast into the coals for the better part. More present was the ration of raw maize we allowed us for that was all we carried. On the sea we dwindled. Four days floated with Peñalosa and Tellez with our direction unguided by any noted stars no story comes to us from the heavens except they will always be there in the heavens above our float and drift above our any way. Dwindled down to the weeds we would have eaten if such was able to us. I've looked over the sides to see what might vanish there and into the sanded ocean I look down in there and at times I see whole lands of fish arranging them into shapes clouded and of a single head and at times I see only the dusted sand hove up from the beds gushing clouded and colored tan with no meal inside it so I ladle my thin arm into this tan and I rest my face on the deck edge and the tar we made my face upon it my thin arm into the sea to ladle from it some sign of why to go to keep us all here and collecting myself back into myself I can not send a view of me to these men in any way other than in full hand and so I gather what has been left to me in this and I call the direction and I call the current is warm and so we are on a good stream known to charts who say the warm stream carries all boats to safe land I call this to the men with my thin arm into the sea and it is their own despair who hauls it in.

It's as such we sail or drift us in this sea who calls our path. The maize in its own lessening. How could the sky in day see fit to spend us like it does?

This in turn is answered. The gathered clouds. The wind who moves a bird against its usual wing into a tumble. The wave who begins to have a tip crested turned over into a brief witness the lip of what's coming. A still wind over the tips enough to move the smell of what's coming on to us and then a wind rises gusted at times and risen into the unwelcome.

Then it is upon us. The slack we laid out unlong to hold us between the periods. Our rafts in climb and fall to this uplifted sea and in time our rafts until then tied but apart come apart entire and we no longer drift with Peñalosa and Tellez but instead it's us together rafted alone the sea again foully sketching the route. Stove away from them and again whimmed out to sea our Lord I cast again to thee the sole why of all our days we are a crew upon this combined by you alone to serve please tell us what it is so the wrack we moil through can somehow depict itself to mean some any plainness. Waves up crested and a wind gusted blown our heads even with our hands up to our ears come blasted lambasted near ruined and such is the smallest of our cares. The sea with us. The land no mention of it to us. The sea surrounding a man it is this man who knows how truly dire it is. Tumbling on land would now be good joy. Set here it's what our deaths appear as. And the news of us goes down with the near last man who gathers the cries of that one last man.

That's as such. The weather his victor. But us we can come ungiven to this.

We've wintered this, against a season. The cold shedding even more damn upon us. The men give in and begin to give out. Falling upon each other as dummies happen. Separated and thrown to, our hope was rested somewhere and the men fell into the poses of fallen dreg.

The sun was setting and the cold was there with us and the weakness of the men was all there was. Stacked men thinned out and upon each other. Their last arm put to use to hold on and not fall off the sides. It was a chore to just lift my sight to see them. And only I could see this. For it was only myself lifted up by the moon and one other who stood us yet. And it was the helmsman who steered us that night until he could no longer for he believed that in that night he would not continue to the dawn with holding his life with him. I took the tiller such as it was and guided us or so. And when the moon was high I went to our helmsman to see if his life was still with him and he stirred up to me and breathed. The sea around us more still now. And he talked to me of how he'd gotten. Feeling good enough to steer again. Our men a broken wrack strewn out there under moon light. He rose and took the tiller and I sat down shot through with stars who up above us held there in witness to our all.

We visit our life just once. It could rain down or it could sun a string of days or an unended ease could be what days you live in but I come to believe we visit our life just once this only one time in which we live, the string of days entire from one until the end. Inside this now I live with my body underneath the sky the stars there I would bet the stars set up there in measure of what we do and pourn down from the moon is my revital. I'm as wracked as any man here and I toil more and eat less and my charge demands that I lift us to the next day and so it is I underneath the moon the other men have fallen upon each other in what could be close to giving in as a body spells its coming day and sapped to the utmost lands where it might and I the moon addresses and it is I the moon floods up with sand for what's upcoming so that I may guide in some way these rafted men who pell-mell upon each other like blown twigs I lie here standed to that task our Lord I become the one who gathers them in to proceed us all into the. Could I call out my desire to be finished to no longer have to witness the men in shapes so drawn and beyond the fetch of hope? What was possible was aside that and my invigor in night my hands on gunwales or so my solemn moon has come on to breed in me the sons of light and the sons in me of the trick who heals me I tread here alone it's mine evening sky alone.

Dawn's gray line just barely seen. My heart wants only some minor hue or red there along the limit just a low sign past the gray what I and we the men we need is a fleshing of the range I please ask it now. What we've been sweltering through until this could forget even this slight color given as a brief sketch of what upcoming goodness could unfurl.

As if the day was some savior opposed to night but a body with its heart comes to believe in a thing such as the dawn such as the new coloration such as the redness of the morning. Hope is in the dance of these wishes.

Shore seemed close for the sound it brought. So we did a sounding and we dropped a corded stone into the sea until the cord was slack and we were in seven fathoms near the shore and as such we mended our course seaward until the light inside a day fell down upon us. The lone horme I held to was to row us from the shore and so I got myself against the land and with my good arms we sended us out to where it was almost safe and it was so until the wave rose up who would then carry us that length of which back to land.

The wave lifted up our boat and men with such an arm that it brought us all down upon this roven shore with men woken up from brutal slumber and exhaust to come falling into the earth with sure notions of the end of their own days. Spreaded out on the shore of a breaker near rogue the men landed. Arranged in a queerness in the sand. Brought awake and to bear once more on the state of what and the state of his self his body risen from deep beyondness to again view the stark drawn outline of his body inside the world his body a twigged remnant up against the nature of a day so much more stout than he. So more ready to continue as if the weather and the sea waves had a mind and that mind was set to go on and its eyes were open and direct upon you unblinking almost in savor of the turmoil it hands out. Us gullied out on the worn maps of Him sunken down into the grooves cut deep by all who came before and augured into the sand of their own claim.

On land the wrack of us scrabbled to the hill up from where we landed. Some bluff at best. The standed crawling. The voices of us only vague notions into the muttered ears who caught the sand. I want to lend hands to men but my hands are only few. I tug men. A dragger of the body from the beach.

Some men have the build yet to scratch up firewood. This fire beckons and this fire should be a notion of camp or a notion of the lee side of wrecking us but the fire instead it tells us I am only a briefness a pale net cast out just this once for you and even in day will I not be here for you I am brief and I gauge how you all are assisted.

Half walking half crawling to the fire where we roasted what was left of the maize and rainwater pools were found for us left here by our Lord for to feed us our revival almost a thing breasted into shape to note an actual life was lifted from the deep fuck we found ourselves in.

It was Lope de Oviedo who brought his body weller than the rest. His health a near marvel and so I sent him across the bluff to a tree that he would find that was tall and climb the tree and reach a version of us. The land. The slope. The color of the canopy and what he could tell. He set himself directly onto this and went toward a stand of taller trees. From where I was it was clear which tree to get a self up into but once inside the stand it was Lope de Oviedo who looked up and from where he was there was a tree who had a foothold and many more laid upward it was this tree he fled up into and learned that we found ourselves on land that was an island. From where he treed himself he also learned or so that ruts in the ground told an indication that cattle roamed here and so to Lope de Oviedo it seemed we were on the land of Christians.

Knowing in my belly that this finding was untrue I sent him out again to better ken the mix we found ourselves near death in to perhaps view a road or some other trail a man might walk on if he was at all in the braces of husbandry or at least my terrible insides spoke to me and so Lope de Oviedo wended out into the island of his Christians to find a road.

The sun its own agent, I could feel the sole of our Lord in great restraint upon us though what He weighted upon us was so dire, in our Lord I persevere I claim to only persevere if given lungs enough. Then Lope de Oviedo went back into those trees but watchful of any danger as if this was something gauged and planned to catching of harm a thing on cue. So wandered he went and fell upon a trail that men had made in this sanded ground which led to houses made by Indian men but they had gone from there and he did not know why there was this abandon. So he went in there and rooked a pot of theirs and a small dog and some goatfish. Before his return with this great sum we sent out a search party for his goneness was far longer than we thought it could have been. And it was his search party who told again that Lope de Oviedo had been tailed by three Indians and engaged them in gestures obscene and primitive and altogether remote from any common cant among each. So gone of any share between them Lope de Oviedo and the search party returned to us with no scathe but along the same bank against the sand were the Indians who tailed them and they waited a distance off so to view us from there but it was not far off we could see them as they waited in a trio of men who had a wig of health around them and the golden sand they waited on caught the light of the day and sloped down to the sea where the forever waves of the sea came up and fell there on the shore and these men of health of stature of sun-colored arms and nourish they looked upon us there as a commanding tableau upon our grim diorama some concocted scene of misery where men could only rest and not rise for they could not rise and the trio waited there looking over their shoulders at us and between our parties a strip of golden beach lighted by the Lord above us the waves on lap their bows rested there in the sand. We assembled pell-mell though not six of us could stand to account for us as an expedition though wandered we came branded by the script we tote alongside and we as men were haggard and less supreme than they were on the beach their shoulders holding gazes upon us and tanned hides they without plan displayed to us as their mute banner of a bigger arm but still as an arm in reserve we waited there with them not far off and soon there was a hundred of them with tools of archery and then it was two hundred men of archery and if it was up to us it would have been a certain thing but instead it was not up to us for we could not rise and to see to ourselves was a farce and to advance us upon the sand between us was a farther camp we lived in which was the next and if my Lord has issue with any of this course please interrupt or fathom or what comes truly following.

Without script or specie we went to them the Inspector and I. It was clear we could not harm any for the way and manner we held ourselves no arm of us could betray this. Ripe with beads and bells we approached them as such. Our gesture from a suite of such unknown to them was meant to cause in them to know we were broke of all meals to know we neared some ended way. Also was our gather of them, if we stood on ground or if there was a notion that in the night we would be set upon and without means to defend we could be shuttled off aside as their night plan for us. We lifted up the beads and the bells we had for them and they in turn each gave me an arrow and in a script unknown to both they had us know they would return in the morning with food for us. So we all on the beach rested our bodies for we did not even have strength to muster any distrust of them it was all true and we must rest tonight.

The moon low on its table it began upward though small and shed its white and blue down. The men on the beach some had not moved since landing and instead of causing us to know I thought of them resting instead of a man who was now dead on the sand nearby. The night passed, the moon cresting slowly with its faint white and blue, the men in writhe or fugue but I could not hear them for my entrustments – my sway upon the course they led and how it was upon me as I know it is upon me to build a guide for us all to get up to.

And as if I had sketched this for us in a wisebook they returned in the morning. We had slept an unsound night. Among some it was certain we would be cut apart into food this morning or at best enslaved and some counted us among the smashed heads for the versus of the both of us all I held the murmurations into the night wind who blew among us that night go through us and blow and I will meet you in the next day.

So they came. And us ensanded so little could we act our wills. Come to us I commanded though to no one save our Lord are we not in congress. Come to us. Our spirits rose up in a false cloud to defend us and in mock war though mock for us we laid remained our bodies in good decline. You see me risen at the fore, yes, our Lord? So they came. Through the early morning and the mizzle they came at us slowly and crossed the land between us with their jugs of water and their fish and with their roots they dug up for us at great expense of hardship to them.

And it was that we accepted this to us and feasted on the fish and drank fully and heard or saw in motions of the hands and arms how difficult it was to dig this root so deeply was it stuck to its parent that it was almost enough to not retrieve it.

Our bodies became well under the care of them over days in which the fish and water and this dug root was brought to us. We became enough to stir. We became almost good men again almost able and the men of us who would die they did so among us.

In our rejuvenate their women came to us in the day and their children came also to see us to view what kind of man washes up here. Is this the man who washes up here? Little more than foam who cunts a wave? They spied a weary company. Dire but recovering. And days to follow the women and children and men returned with the glorious what we needed to again stand upward and commote.

So well we became due to them that we minded us to dig up our raft from out of the sand dune where it was buried and we did this without clothing for the task was great and without robe was best and so we dug up the raft and looked upon it. We gave the raft a brief inspect its logged wood soaked the binding cords loose and those were set taut. We gathered vessels the Indians had brought us and there was a mat of dried fish and naked we launched the raft with us upon it. We had become healthy and so we set out into the sea again. Repaired men destined for the better following. Casting ourselves into the tough spew.

And we not two crossbow shots from land were hit by a wave who lifted us up into an unnatural shit. The coldness of it and the nakedness of us caused us all to drop what it was we held if it was an oar or it was a leather bag of bells it all went seaward no matter and then a next wave enfucked us back onto the beach where not less than one gather of time we had embarked and spread us with violent deal back to the shore. The Inspector and two men clung to the raft and they soon came to live under the waves as dead men who sink to the unlighted room where we all go but theirs a water room they were pulled down by the raft and died. The other men had landed on the rough shore and I was among them. I go among them. Our men. With no clothing as if we had described the day of our birth as bare to God as though we could count our bones on account of our thinness. My Lord I've gotten to the succumb but I've not enfallen to it.

I will always lift me to the next. This isn't guessed.

Again deep ensanded. November or so shut in around us and us as bare as I have just said in this. May then allow us now the moment, us all, to lay up such a claim that since May I have not but eaten a thing aside the maize which we are now bereft of and in those days of men in dine on the horse we brought who then starved and trod and with some greater wisdom as the sun lights an afternoon act it was the horse who had both eyes open to what we tried to walk us through. And we did not. And we do not.

Starved and bones for all the sand to see. It is us on the banks of this outer land. Our bodies thrown. And added to this upon us was a north wind who began to blow and this bended in on us and onto our thinness that neared us to death as close as we could at all without us ended entire there.

It is in a when like this our Lord lends us sayings or ways to describe the sea or firmament or the color of the crabs who sideways across the beach or how men look for each other when it is the utmost to look for his self and our Lord is singing this now to me and He sings this to me alone so that our condition comes down to a slowness and the men seem to lose their sound to me and their pace is like a man under the sea who sounds like a man under the sea but we are on the beach all of us who remain who were not sent down to the sea floor we shamble unsteered on this beach and I am here our Lord I have been lifted to hear you sing and I have become tall and my listen is clear it is but one listen to what you sing my tears are not for the deaths we come up to but they are tears for you our Lord for you have set us here as such in such deep want there must be some untold sins for which we have not yet fessed I can not know for how deeply we are left here in strand of all we could have but it is you our Lord who sings this noted song on how the day has just begun and how so rich it has been to now before the sun has gotten up above us yes and how back on this beach without any of us with some clothes any longer we are washed up here but washed all the same and in this new unburden will I not fall into the arms of a man and become taken by the very next what happens that could might.

Then God commands us to find a spark He's hidden in the sand we landed in. An ember we left there without a thought from the night before we cooked on or heated us at least. We behold the ember as it is the one commanded us to find it so our Lord has again sent us delivery from the sins we must weigh out the sins we must account us for the sins who went and put us here where on the sand we tumbled got thrown duly crammed into this beach shoved into and down as much as any man could. This ember beheld up and carried into the fires we builded to Him, the fires we build up to our Lord and the heat of these fires is the deepest touch our Lord could send down to us ensanded and broke of all goodness of the land. And we fall over ourselves to count the sins we've accrued and the sins we could assume from the man who sits next to thee beside the fire he so as a man also enburdended with the sacks of misdeeds to sum up we fall over the man who from the sides of our fugue moments depicts for us the one who could gather what we've fucked up and net it into some fetchable hove. The man beside me and the man beside me I could not envision his falseness but I must gather him both I must tell. We moved our pity. We shed tears who only come counted by our Lord so builded in the tears we come up with are the deepest tears the ones most held and counted. We were this then. A shambled weep huddled to the fire we came up with and us without guard or wrap those both unthinkable then.

HOW THE INDIANS WEPT FOR US

From the treeline in sunset when we had come to the moment in a day when a body howso wracked sets itself to begin the night it gives itself to the lulls laid out ahead and then from the treeline the Indians began to come to us. It was unknown to them that we had given the sea a try and that the sea had not accepted us but hucked us back duly and stern. And to see us so benched and without vim and far worse than how we seemed that very morning they withdrew for their superstitions must have held up great mosaics as to what had come down upon us and the why and we had been reduced by the heavens to what we were so they retreated to avoid a similar reckoning into the woods from who they came.

Unannounced even to myself I came to my feet and went to them. We could not this dusk let them fall back to where and I called to them with our sounds who do not match and I brought my arms up to them and they were surrounded by a fear they cast inside them and through a set of gestures I could not ever do again I put some gestures together to convey our raft was gone and that men went down with it dead and that our Lord had sent the sea rogue to pitch us back here with bad haste and they themselves the Indians saw two of our men on beach sand with life entire gone because they became dead there with us and saw the rest of us getting toward that same death with no hedge between us and that.

On seeing us so without shevel and broke of footholds and cast drifted in our own ensanded deathwalk into the unlighted room these Indians of so massive arm builded from the sun's bestowance to the body these Indians after a time did divine my gestures and once this was so the

Indians brought their bodies inward and down over to us and drawn in as such they wept. The Indians sat with us and brought out such a lamentation it could be heard for leagues if there was an ear out there. The bended river and the crescent lake who bends and the men and women there would hear this lamentation. We there ensanded could gather in these arms the entirety of them and combined was us lamenting, weeping to the pit of us how deeply we drew our sorrow together and knit us blended into a common wail, the heavens could have noticed. We all wept in a loudness only deep shedding of all what measures us can allow. What they lacked in common wisdom and reason and because their brutishness was main and their refine-ment was no more than nothing it was their base ways who spelled out to us how deeply we had fallen. That these crudes could weep for us at all gave light to truly how deep we'd come, how our sins were so buried in us and we now for these sins shelled it out.

What I asked next of our men was that we go with the Indians to their houses. And the men who had been in New Spain forbade even the vote for if we went with them it was sure that they would hatch us into what they offer to their idols or their gods who might have been drawn somewhere in the sand for them to revere and us on their altars cut up and several and so no it was not even a thing to consider. But I had become an agent for our being and I had assumed the yoke of us though none of them could indeed post witness to the handing of it over and did not come to understand what I already gathered about us and so I deemed it was a must to go with them and that our death was near to us and either or what ever path we ended on our selves were near ended as such and it was a coin who we tossed and each end of it was unwanted. I chose for us against an even choice at all to do so and I chose for us to go with them to be among what I had chosen for us at all. This news to the Indians brought them a grand pleasure and they bade us to wait there on this sand and they would return.

Some of the men prepared themselves to be shandied into the next world by way of an Indian who brings down hacks to hack us apart and some of the men were too weak to even fret them up to anything much and so they looked at the sand and the trees and the waves continuing on the beach and the sea who in some way was the same sea that fell upon our home in Spain and they heard the sound of the waves on the beach continuing in air and smelled the air of where we were and considered this place undrawn on any map and my eyes have seen this land and it will be the final land I see in this life and our Lord has brought us to an ending here no one could have guessed for us what an untold ending it will be on us and some men with the strength left to them attempted to assemble weapons out of the raw dirt and branches ready to them as if they would fend or begin to set out against these sure giants and it was only they who felt this was a path enough to build into the dance they lit into and some of the men did not alter from what they had been for days and for weeks to then as if unchanged they would set venture into this next and some of them men which included me and unsure if men else these men which might have been only me we ended a prayer to our Lord to seek witness for the thanks we gain to thee and to pardon us for the unseen jacket of sins we must have gathered up up until then and we went aside to fulfill something as it was enormous dire given our then fix in which we found us it was dire to congress at least this once upon the sins we must have gathered and upon the guide we'd been handed down throughout and upon the many splits in our path we could have opted elsewise upon and upon the very wave after wave sended down to us who bended our route and upended us back into some refucked encampment and isn't it we who fold in your good aims and who spend toiling beyond counted days on paths enlightened by you our Lord we have chosen again from the said routes laid out for us and chosen as only we can with our rude means and we've come to give ourselves over to these men who we now trust with our many hearts into a wholly unknown and then after ending this prayer we found if there were men to be tended to and how to gauge this was unsure and then the sun began down into the west and painted the weather with reds and hues that we had seen before in dusk the nights before this on end there we waited on the beach for the Indians to return or to not return it was either way we'd be there on this beach and so it was it was us until then.

It is the night. See us then.

They return for us. See us then.

We've come up to death there on the beach and we have given ourselves over to the next, and see us then.

An excitement houses them, they've come back to do a certain thing and to set upon it see us on the beach near death so to see in their return.

It is against us to oppose what comes to us, against our manner to stand here, to so very emprouden us, see us here the eyes we've kneeled to see us I've asked to see us here for how we've been lifted from the beach.

They've come for us and they take us from here from the deep sand and predicament come gathered us and begin to bring us into another night it is a night away from the beach and a night into some new where. We are from the beach and it is unclear if we are in the way of where they live or if we are in the way of some flay of us to remember us into a different corpse and so we go with them as death was as near as our dear saviors and we are taken by them into the woods.

Their good arms convey us. We are brought. An ensanded path. We feel enchanted along to where they are.

We sing a new voice if we can sing.

Knowing our health was ending they had prepared for us some fires along the route and at each fire we waited and became warm and then we were lifted by them as if we did not have ground underneath us and went us to the next fire deeper into the woods on toward their houses. When they saw that we had regained some movement or that our eyes had become alive enough they lifted us again and flew us to the next fire. And in this way we reached their houses where they had prepared a house for us with another group of fires inside it.

Soon thereafter they began to dance and parade and proclaim things into the air with upheld arms and a look of thanks and this dance lasted all night but for us there was no dance and even there was no rest for most of the men waited for the moment when these able men would storm us and undo us all to the bones.

In the morning they came with fish and with roots for us to eat and with water and we began to regain somewhat our bodies who'd gone to the lip of that deep gulf and had seen into the gulf with his own eye how near we had been to fall inside it. And after more fish had come to us from them we even began to think they might not undo us for their rituals or instead to provide themselves with us.

THE BAUBLE AND FOUND

The morning of the fish and roots I saw an Indian and attached to him in a way I find unable to convey was an item from men who were Christians and this item I knew could not have been from the last of which we brought with us on our boat for I had long hours to assess what was in that leather bag we used to hold our pieces we traded and in there there was nothing as such I know because I looked in and spent the time with them as we floated on the open sea and the men diminished around me and in that leather bag there was nothing like what he wore upon him in an untold way and so I approached him. We came together and in gestures I sought to wonder where he came to wear such a bauble and in gestures and his mouth in sounds he told me in terms defined as such that there were men like us farther back in these woods and that they had given him the bauble.

I sent two Christians and two Indians to find them and this was a small task as they were also looking for us and had been told of us by these Indians. Our Lord had weighed the sins of all of us and had come up with this enactment it was the captains Andrés Dorantes and Alonso del Castillo and all of the men who were with their boat. On seeing us it did not occur to us our current health might aback them but that is what, and they did recoil for we were abundant in our lack and in our frailing and they fell into a depth of sorrow for us for they did not have a giving thing in them for us at all and as we met so we did remain and us with all our bodies in an open fuck to the sun and his senses.

Some days before it was Dorantes and Castillo and they had come upon a wave who went and put them into an over-turn and so they went over but none of the men on their boat were died of it and they reached shore without a loss. Their raft was also near able and hauled up onto a dune.

And so as there were men able to continue it was planned we should do so and on the remaining raft. It was a must. We took the further curtains apart and gave sight to what is next. The men who could not go on would remain and when they were brought back to health they would continue along the coast as their bodies would take them and then God our Lord could send them to the land of Christians or he could not and it was up to them together to go deem it.

And as we put this to consider, Tavera who was a quiet man and nimble he Tavera died.

And as we put this to consider, the raft we took to be our good ship it went and slid down with a tall wave back into the sea and sank of its own choosing.

And as we put this to consider, weighed out was our health and how our naked skin was unsuited to travel on land in that late season and our food a thing of wonder as well as how to carry it if it was an actual – we felt conspired upon by the heft I've laid out and ending us to the plan it was come to as this – we'd winter here for there was no other means to get us on.

Also deemed was that four of us would go the way of Pánuco for it was believed there was a river there we had seen the charts of this and a town where Spain had built a town there and when the four do arrive abundantly carried by the winds of our good Lord they will convey the state of us here on this island and word will reach them of us and our deep needs. So these four were chosen because they were great swimmers and had been judged the best to survive the way of Pánuco if in fact there was a fording to be done with only the one body each had. Along with these four there was an Indian from the island who was nearby. He went with each as well. And so they set off and they give themselves over to the possible next.

Waited in the houses of the Indians our bodies drawn down and few of us could use his own. Them who could did gather with the Indians the root we used to eat. And then the skies loaded in them a darker hue. Our four Christians had been gone only a few days and waited there we held our eyes up to notice the view and it was the cloud builded up into a talling group who darkened and a wind began to move down from north of us. The nights began to colden and we shook in night and kept our bodies together and traded in the night the outermost place to be so that in time the ones surrounded would move out and resit in turn until dawn.

There was a frost about then. The sun was hidden still behind that unmoving dark cloud steady above us so the sun was hidden from us. The cold moved around with its metal voice we didn't have some place to go from it. The sky was upended and storms came down on us in deep heads we could not keep a fire lit against them. The Indians could not pull up the roots we ate the days were so blown. Our shelters what they were did little and our bodies met again some foe setted down by our Lord to see how we tested to them.

This could not still be our sins we must account for and weigh up against. There could not be any left to trade I am as certain of that as we are fucked here.

To us then so death was visited. It was must to be. The men and young Indians began to perish and they died and women died and two slaves who were held by these Indians rooked from another group and fed little for what they labored they died together in the tree they embraced and Christians died with their bodies strung out and cracked.

Corral, Sierra, Diego Lopez, Gonzalo Ruíz, and Palacios. These five men were encamped on the beach away from us and away from the Indians and they began to perish and when a man died of them they took his body and it was used to feed the men who remained. As each man died he was consumed by them who lived until there was one remaining and when he died there was not another man to enfooden him.

The Indians came to know of this and it was seen by how they went about with this news inside them it was an act they forbade in utmost so as to leave this to them almost unsayable. Our lives such as they were were now even more hemmed.

Of the eighty Christians who landed on that island from all camps and boats there now were left eighteen. Death following into camp another three of our men died. And after we had dwindled to fifteen the Indians became ill with a sickness that became inside the belly and spread outward and soon half of these Indians had died of this cause. And for this we were held to blame as the ones who set free among us all this sickness or had in some way abled this illness in our will to do so upon them and so they came to us to end us for this.

I had been given to the care or possession of one of the Indians and it was through him I came to know their ways and in the movements of our hands and through the pitch of our sounds I had also handed over some idea of our ways.

When the Indians who had decided to end us for the sickness we caused they believed it was the Indian who cared or possessed me stood up with his body and brought his body between them and us to halt them from what they came to do and he did reason that if the Christians had caused the illness then why would they also bring the illness to themselves and to perish off their own men for there were only few left of us who lived then. Why did we use this power against us? But we prepared to be riven up and left out for birds to get at so the mood had been drawn for us and then our Lord God rode in in his certain way and caused the mood to ease and consider what had become our case. And our Lord God then had them turn away and to believe the best course would be to let us be and so we were.

The storms kept on in continued wind and cold and them who went out in the weather to get food it was them who returned lost of any catch or root. And so we left the island of Malhado which is what we had come to name this place and in canoes the Indians who had come to be my lot we crossed from Malhado to the mainland where it was known to have bays in which an oyster could be handed up out of the sea by the many.

On the mainland there is little firewood and gnats are like a sounded blanket who moves in slow turns around you in night and in day and on top of beds of oyster shells the Indians build their houses of woven reeds and if fortune or some spell bestows an animal skin to them it is this skin upon which they'll sleep in night on. And although the water is near poison and the hunger we carried was severe and the mourning for those new lost to them was is and the cold was run along with us they did not put halt to the dances and to the songs which had a deep place in their ways and they did not put halt to the lifted ceremonies who mark the taller days of the year. And it was here we stayed with the Indians who were my lot for some three months until we met the end of winter and then we went back to the seacoast where blackberries for near one month is what we had for food.

She lay dying there her back up against a tree and it was the only recline for leagues. She had ears still and they took in the silence and the sound the sun makes on the sand and the palm fingers up overhead the whisper they lend down and what a mote of animal arms were there. She'd been left there a grandmother is what I took from her story and her story was a line of gestures and the way her eyes moved about it. This is how these Indians put each other when they become old and unable to do much to gather roots or dig or haul the pieces of their houses taken apart to travel. It was all I could do then to lay by. There was a notion not letting me leave the woman, it was as if my body though wracked and taut as I've been and wanting for almost all its store even then the most of what I needed was to be with her in her what seemed there against a tree in shade or so her dying. There was a need I can not say for why it was but her there and her eyes looked up to between the sun and shade the palm fingers set down on the front of her inside her what must have been to her own insides the final beats of her walk among them all. It's not able for a near soul to go and leave a body alone I'm sure of this and so I sat with her in sun and fingered shade and when her tough skin shuddered I too was with her in that and in her night stories I could gather what her daughter and sons and the sons of them did able at and who was held dearest to her it was clear the way her eyes went and her breathing told a story about her dearest one the girl who was young and was swept one night up into the moon river in full run and she was carried out to set the moon with it out to sea and her breathing and her back the way she held herself told a story of the others and of her own knotted past from what I could gather and in night her shudders and her silence was a story she doled out to me together we and the palm fingers and she leaned there and no other of her people went to her but instead it seemed already she was gone to them I was unable to see how.

She died by nature who it was to come leaving us without her. And our men have died up to now and death it has been a steady hand with us to now and duly measured we've all been guided near some death or so. So our nature is to walk and our nature is to keep by the sitting of an elder in her shudders and in turn to walk.

This casting of the no longer useful arms came to us Christians then as an equal law – it was told to us in no words the useful man has a post here and otherwise is there any reason we all feed you? And it was offered in no words that to be of use to them we should employ our powers to heal sick men and do this.

The young elders they did this healing by the blowing of the healer onto the ill and through this a cure is somehow sent over to the sick. When they came to us to enlist our powers in this healing art it was beyond us and we told them in words who had no truck inside what hearing they'd. Then our cost for this was that following days we had no food and food was kept from us and so we came to know the dire sides of what was laid out to choose and what each meant to us. So brought again to some brink of health ourselves no longer nourished but instead in further dwindle for the blowing on the sick we did not embrace. So held in turn again we ebb and blow healing to whomever needs it.

But it was our resist who brought to us an Indian man he stooped low to give us something and it was this. That it was not the man or the blowing breath to cure an illness but instead we do employ the tools of our world and if we claim to not know how to use them then one did not know what we claim at all. For the stone we use when heated and placed on the belly of an ill man will cure the man no matter who placed it there. And by using the seed pods of the biggest trees who shed seeds in a pointed ball who falls almost all year and so this seed ball is crushed apart and the lint of it is rubbed into the front arms of an ill man and it does not depend on the man who rubs the seeded lint it so becomes the healing of an ill man for the seed pod and the heated stone it all has a healing built into it from the fact of it itself. And so do not believe that you're unable to cure men for it is not your own tell but instead the tell of what is found in the stone and in seeds who send us into the goodness we live us for. And so the Indian man no longer stooped and walked from us as if he was a chart himself on how we might. His back to us and his skin away from us with each step we left and it was further shaded in how these Indians came to value things and for us we included this in our thinking and our hunger and our ancient habit to go on.

So up we took it and studied the methods they had with them and also built onto those methods some of our own as if the hot stones and the seedpods and the blowing could be well augmented and we mixed in these fabricates. The Ave Maria and the Pater Noster was also canted with the blowing and these we trusted and held dear as the actual charms who did the work assigned.

When it was time for the ill to come to us we used our new hand in healing and with our own addendums we went about what the young elders would do but with cruder means for the crudeness of us was yet of the utmost and our nakedness held us far from what we believed to be the way some physician would carry himself to the ill but even so we counted or at least were robbed of health and seated by our own default and they came to us in their illnesses. They came to us with skin illness and with torn backs and they could not breathe and a sharp rock put itself into the foot of one boy up to the bone or it was an oyster shell or an elder came to us and he saw twice what should be seen and his thoughts were shotted through with pain whose day was always on. No matter what the downfall we could first blow upon them and then sing out the Ave Maria as best we could recall but we recited and we blew our healing breath or so upon them and if there was a grain of doubt we hauled out some Pater Noster and laid it there upon the pine needle floor or it was a sandy floor and our Lord God who looks down upon us in some way he so duly assisted us, yes?

And he came to us the tallest man they had and although they did not have a lord among them it was seen how this taller man was held to them. His tallness made him a rangy man and he moved like a spider in the cold. His head was stooped for it could only hang from where it was and his step was halted by the bending his legs had to do each step and he shifted to us his arms set to his sides the long arms hanged against him and like the praying bugs we've seen it has more angles than seem to be of his use and his front arms come up now to note something he's said to us we bend us together to try to know his say. He leans he can not sit with us and so he leans against a closer tree and his hands at the ends of his spindles try to tell us of his illness. His hands shake against a will to keep them from doing so and so his command of himself is small and he has a reed who passes through his under lip and through his nipple in through a hole he's made there is a reed there too and it is thick as two fingers and from his man is hanging one stone tied there with a fiber he must have twined up by hand his shaking hands they conveyed the story already told. We had seen this state in our own land ago and it was such that a man who was ill with this habit was sent to the monastery where he was sent to be cured by our Lord God but we knew that it was so the stricken man would be forgotten and out of our pouring thoughts about him and the news of his death when it came was taken in with a sweet bitterness for the day was dark and yet the day was a rock lifted off us all. And his spindle arms they rustle and his cripple tells us one thing but he finds he believes another and it is yet up to us to put our hands on him and cast out this tremor and lay him back into the men who pull oysters from the sea and dig roots and haul houses to the next. Fuck us all for what we're in I tell the sun who sets on us then. What good is possible from our simple Ave Maria and from the borrowed acts we've seen done by the young Indian elders we now use to send hope in some direction near to them? He leans there his tree a solid pole he counts on. His eye is not as much to ask of us a cure but it is to tell us only of his state and that it is so and nothing else. Some pact is written then? We guess as always. To spell out what comes is nothing we could even tend to now. And so the ground between us is ready for us each but we both hold us where we are and allow an unknown judge to decide or allow olden habits to intrude on us there and so the habits or judges or it is our Lord who decides the stillness of the day is not done yet and we remain to each other some message to be read.

Sunup. We convene among us all naked and setted to the day. The rhythm of them. Of us. A conference, and some are decided.

The Indians and Andrés Dorantes and Alonso del Castillo and the rest of the Christians who were living they all prepared to go and it was unknown to where and they set off and were gone. But I alone was lended to the Indians who spoke and went on in their own manner and they brought me to the mainland with them.

It is there on the mainland with my Indians that I fell ill into a depth I have not known and so death was close to me and death did not have much to cross to reach me and I did not have one thing I could muster against this and so I was certain of the end of me. I was broke of any hope to be living soon.

The rest of them were on the island of Malhado. In my void it was Dorantes and Castillo and on the island they gathered all Christian men and there were fourteen Christian men. And so to continue us all in the way of Pánuco and to the town of Pánuco there, Dorantes and Castillo brought these Christian men back to the mainland and it was the belief that this collection of men was all who remained of our boats. Twelve men crossed back to the mainland for two of our Christians were too ill and unwell to trek and so these two men Jerónimo de Alaniz and Lope de Oviedo remained on the island of Malhado and Dorantes and Castillo and the rest crossed back to the mainland and they came to me where I was being held by my Indians.

My illness was to me dire and this can not be mapped enough how close death came to me then and I held little hope to convince an else. I was laid there in sticks and sand they mounded to my sides in the way they set to care for ill men and my days were unknown to me. I had days then but I could not know how many or what was held inside the days for my Indians and I remained there cupped in that mounded sand and my water went out from me and the color of the sky was something other than what it must have been and painted for me there was a different day who resembled little of the day at hand and I pulled my skin over me to keep warm and it was told to me that I drank water when it was not so much brought to me as left there in absence.

Dorantes and Castillo came to me as such. They were the shapes of men but sizes ungoverned by reason so hands were giant and feet and heads with mouths were of a size no man could harbor and bended to the side they came to me and I could not move from my sand to greet these giants and my mouth was filled with itself. There must have been a piece to connect them all with what I knew for my heart recalls this mostly, my heart saw them as the men I came to be with for long and they returned to me as men I know. The mist around their odd shapes held up and they teetered with giant eyes and teeth and I could not wipe away the lens who rewrote their visit to me. So they told me I'm told they mean to set off in the direction of a river to continue along the coast and away and to bring me of course to go with them.

I must have done little more than drag an arm against my bunker there. My eyes did not look back I'm told to where the travel was noted. To where the men waited. I could have shifted or put out a leg from where it was to get signal to the men but what my tongue was doing in my head was meant to do that and that whole try was unseen and I could do little to alter the trade we all had. And so my sanded eye and my head rested there on twigs and my open mouth who went and kept on for the whole of it they took to be my unable to go with them and that I would soon be held by death and I would remain and they could set off to what river was ahead.

Then for what I could not recall even for some outline of what it might have been like at the time they were gone and away and my eye must have followed them for as long as it could have done and the big hands they held were setting off and my sanded mound was a cup I rested in to see them off.

THE YEAR OF CUT HANDS AMONG THESE INDIANS

They had gone and I was too ill to follow. I was made to stay with my Indians for almost a year and in this year my illness sent some of itself away from me and I was again almost able and I waded in the shallows for the root we ate and in the rushes I waded when I was able and I pulled up what we needed to live and in this doing so it was my hands who came enfucked of it and cut up and raw to the next edge the next sharper blade I let myself do the next person's bidding but it was my own skin who paid it off and to pay it I dug each day for the root and the rawness and baldness of these fingers I went down into the rushes and cut them deep and these were my early days with them.

So come to me and embrace this elegy – an elegy of lateness I've come accustomed to.

My año with the heathen my año with the men who scale their lines so distant from mine.

Drawn out the cutted hands. I'm seen of it, pulling up roots in rushes I head back to mats of reeds any soften of the land we're on I welcome.

My Indians live on oyster midden piles laid out in stacks for what mounding I can still not ken. Above the what? As if a rise was good to fend some night pincer night tooth who would do harm. No way to know and I am too in need of food to know what's better. Sunken. I'd make an oyster midden if I could.

It's not possible to know I'll be here for a year. Mine año among them. My body without cover and in the reeds who cut me open with the broken ends of them and edges as if honed to do well against a man.

To leave these Indians I can only plan as much as my awaken hours allow this. When unfed it becomes a longer tale of reaching that good health and so months continue and I go without food and I am sent to dig roots among those reeds and I can tell I am still on the teetered edge of to live or to be denied entry into my own body here on land. Days in need of mending health and calls to our Lord for a notion or some lifted hand or even the shape of a cloud to mean a sign I could take to then build into the way on.

Months ended without my finding any sign and passed into further days marked only by the angles of light and the tallness of the shadows laid down.

156

In a moment my bigness was guessed and my health was up to go at night and to leave these Indians so to bring my self further into the mainland and the woods and the Charruco Indians who trade with my Indians who hold me captive and live deep in the mainland woods. I setted off from my Indians. The full moon guided my step and I continued on in a night way along no path but in brambles and knotted ground. The light sand an almost guide to where, the moon a direction to keep along. I slept a low count in moments when to go on it wasn't true. I laid in sand and some loudness a bug it could have been made the night awake and on I went to go further until I came upon the Charruco in a nearness and in dark and so I waited in my sand until the light to go to them.

IV

I am a hidden man in open scrub I believe I can be hidden laid low against a pricker whose sharp fronds dagger me I'll hide behind to wait out my advance. My dawn in all ways. I'm as if a scar shirted me and I feel only the press of something severe and meant. Wracked still and edged up to broken my body on the end verge and there is little our Lord God can recommend and little our Lord God can lend who could increase my health.

I've waited longer spells. When uncles put wine in them and bade soon return I waited there and tended one fire and set myself up in some manor play I'm cloaked and velvet gowned I've service and windows thick at the bottom and sailed in ships I'm a child captain and I'm roaming seas and wandered against better judge and I come upon the fruits I've heard paintings of from islands only drawn up from madmen's recalled dement I've accustomed to the legs I get at sea the tossing a body comes used to so the moon buys us east and other for the fate of it.

I've in nights longer than this such a spell longer gone paced in halls to wait out the word of another ranked up above me.

And in the true dawn I'm seen I'm on my belly my body is an armadillo tail and my head is up inside the under boughs of a shrub my body is its own dry bird and it's hollowed out I'm seen by an early Charruco his morning comes to me and now it is his body I'm with. He brings himself down into my sleep and I could not judge his meaning for my new day to me and I could not judge his meaning for the bones in me didn't serve my ready so fallen down in health and then so new to my new eyes then and so he came down to me fast and entire to me and set his head at once between my shoulders with his ear and I was then alive to this same day. Like crabs we then both went sideways quick and brief to face each other. His morning eyes and his dyed tassle. Our suddenness and double ghast and our sudden entry to what was between us. Then no one sprang. And then no one of us spoke or brought a hand up. The sand between us ungone into.

I drew into the sand an island outline and I drew what was to me a long coastline and with a twig that I had made into myself with a gesture I showed how the twig came from the island across the inlet and across the rivers near the coast and came to be here this twig who was another me. And with his gesture the Charruco found a separate twig and this twig he became and he placed the twig next to mine and he looked up his eyes having found a bearing in me and our exhibit and he drew a line from those two twigs away from the coast and to the far inland and then he raised his arm and pointed to there and we went in that direction.

Our Lord would protect me in this my next people my next what I walked to. What for He is willing to do my behalf is granted well and there upon is lended at least some minor light. What I walked to I walked inside of this.

Among the Charruco I began ill for days. Then when I was well they set me to a task. In front of me was put a band of snails and also conch pieces who were rubbed into shapes to cut. What was also put there in front of me were the rounded stones we took from inside the oysters who had them and it was only the fewest oysters who built a stone in them and the stone itself was as smooth from any side you viewed it and as round so that on a smooth board this stone would roll in any way you leaned it toward and inside the stone it grew a color who matched the clouds and mixed hues to shape the high clouds who trail out when the wind is at its most telling and these are idols or I could feign guess at what they counted for among them. If it wasn't a tool it must have been a false God. In time another conch was put on there in front of me and it was honed along one curved side to a sharpness which could lay halves to an aloe frond at once. These all were gathered into a mound and were presented to me with a left hand and with the right hand it was pointed in the way of inland and to the continuing coastline where I had not yet been in either way and it was gestured to me that in exchange for what was put in front of me I would trade these things for other things.

164

WHAT FOLLOWED

Followed days set inland followed days within sound of waves headed south in trees along the coast as a trader followed nights went on trails by moonlight if the moon was causing enough light sent down followed days sewing hides enough with tendon sitting on the ground sewing hides into the bag I'd use to truck these conch pieces and these stones from inside an oyster and these pieces of the snail shells to carry in it followed days along the coast for forty or fifty leagues to come upon other Indians who would use the conch shell hones to cut and flay and unbone a thing and they would use an oyster stone to decide what path they would take when the weather turned into winter and oyster stones could also be arranged on a wet frond and the arrange of them on the frond would tell if it was a night to dance and to ask the night to cure them followed nights lost or on a path I'd unknown and there a night sound is made into something more clawed and toothed and in its own way on a hunt and there it was the hand of our Lord the hand who led me to the clearing where I could right again my senses and the hand of our Lord did guide me and I was able to it followed days returned to the Charruco with my hide bag and in it what I traded for and the Charruco would dance when I returned and they brought to me the food they had followed on back to the wooded inlands where red ocher I got from them these Indians inside the woods who were against the Charruco in battle with them and so to move trade between them I passed from one and back an unassigned roam in trade and finding routes followed days on these routes I lie flat to face the puddle and drink from it and I lie there so to thank our Lord God who delivers and provides when I am most in need so that I do not fail so that I find my route forward and to Pánuco so that I remain a man followed days when the light would come and leave sooner and the wind was opposite to me and there was no fire that I was near and gone into the night huddled up to me was me in what I could small myself into against the cold who came followed soon then a route who tailed into the coastal Indians who lit fires at night and who mourned some time I could not know about and held on to mourn inside the shaded huts to moan and take the food left at the open end of each hut when there was food to be left there followed one day crossing back to the island of Malhado and after a time I found Oviedo and he told me Alaniz had died ago and I asked Oviedo to come with me to go the way of Pánuco forward and I could tell him of my travels in that way and how we could get us to there but we must go together so to help each other and now was the season to do this and Oviedo said he was so unwell that he could not go and he could not swim and this was something to cause in him the fear to stay and I tried to move Oviedo to come with me and I would not leave without him and I told him how I would lead him over the swum parts of our travel but he could not be moved to come with me in the way of Pánuco and so followed a return to the mainland and to walk into the trees and trails inside them as a trader followed days of dug roots to eat them with the Charruco who laid out one infirm onto a mat and a boy who was decided he could heal traced a line around the mat and the infirm there he traced a line drug behind him with a stick and inside the line the healer put all his healing but the infirm in that very night passed over into death and the boy who traced a line was put out to sea on a flawed canoe and he became small and small and the men on shore turned a back to him and returned to where the roots were cooking followed days in travel in the way of Pánuco keeping a book inside me of where to cross the inlets and marshes and which estuary led inland or was ended and where there was a tree and what season the tree had nuts on it to pull down followed shells in trade become flint become the chipped edges sharp to cut and tied to the head of a stiff shoot and this was an arrow followed into the rain and a season when the smoke was added to us all around us at night to make a room for us against the flies who would come to you in a blanket of them followed days of digging into the land and digging into the sand below the sea for the roots we could eat and the roots are put back into the land in the hole next to rocks who were in the fire and over the roots inside the hole was covered over and over one night it all waited there in land inside the dug hole until it was upended and the roots again dug out and now the roots were cooked to eat and so we ate them and then went back out to near the holes where those roots had been dug up the day before and we dug up more roots there until there were no more roots there or under the sea in the sand to dig up followed nights of a cold I became to learn I could sleep through although if a dream came in a cold night the dream was also cold and so there was no way to get from it and our Lord God did not deliver me from the cold but he did instead keep me alive so that I could live through the cold and I requested of our Lord God to guide me then and I request his guide in usual and in times I cannot come to fathom his decision for me and if there is some deliver set to come followed by the death of an Indian healer who was a doctor by their means and his body was burned and what was left of him was bone and his bone was crushed between two stones who fit together well for this and his bone was put into a dust and in a wooden bowl this dust and water were added in and

167

stirred so that the son and granddaughters of the healer could drink his bone and keep him alive inside them who survived him in life and his two wives could mourn and starve themselves alone followed in the sea again digging roots where they pass low from the shore under the sand and where I was digging I was digging the day before and knew well there were no more roots there to dig up and so I was low in the sea with my arms down below the water moving in the motions as a man does who digs up roots but I was not digging roots I was almost in the act of it but instead I could look off to where I could recommend myself to our Lord God and to be in his unended mercy and I could look off to where my sins have been kept in sum as it must have been a mountain who builded itself up from the ground to lift the peak of my sins higher this must have been my sins and how there was no end to them and to plane off the sides the mountain rises still for who could I be to lessen it now who could I have become at all over these days and weeks in each season I have ensavaged I have carried weights no noble man would ever bring himself to carry and I have been hit with sticks and with an arrow drawn to my heart I have been asked if I was afraid of it and I have been cut for play by the claws of Indian boys who game upon my drawn blood and on my back I haul wood to cook and eat by and water and I have been sent off into the woods when there were not enough roots or mice to feed on and I was sent off to be one less hunger so I went to the next Indians and who could I be now to lessen the sins I look off to and I could look off to where it was out there on the sea on our rafts when it was decided that no man could help another and that it was all to just be the one who remains by what means at all and if the other rafts by now could have ended any better than ours and I could look off to the bird clouds who bend and race to the one bird who leads the cloud over and I could look off when under the water my arms acted out the digging and so to rest the day followed one late day out by the far edge of us I was with one Charruco to gather wood and we had it piled onto the tendon strap and coming to us was an Indian from a near tribe come out the woods to us there and was in a walk to the Charruco and the Charruco put down his sticks and then he sat down on the ground and the Indian from the near tribe sat down to face him and they were close so that a hand could touch an arm and they both wept entirely as if some great sadness had befallen them both at once between them so they wept on until it became more dusk around us and the Charruco who had with him a pouch with divining stones in it and some food tied to himself and a skin of water the Charruco gave all of these things to the Indian from the near tribe the both of them in full weep yet and they rose and the Indian from the near tribe gathered the food and the pouch and water and he turned and walked back into the woods from where he came and so we gathered more wood and tied the tendon strap around our stack and I lifted it onto my naked back and we returned with it to burn with the Charruco followed into the turns wandered some leagues along the coast the way of Florida and some leagues the way of Pánuco and my hide bag and in it the stones we choose from inside an oyster these stones inside a smaller bag who was builded from the cured gall of a deer in salted oil heated then filled in with these milkstones worn down by all the oyster mouths the hide bag and shell chips and shells who make a wall around the snail and these emptied could dig and cups and move the skin away from the deer body what could also help in this a conch shell or bits of it and these also I had inside the hide bag when some leagues

169

along the coast I could roam to trade and come upon men who welcome my coming and known they prepare an entrance I walk into them and their open lanes they've set out for me to the clearing they've made for me and I go there and kneel down with my hide bag and around me it's them and they come to kneel and it is the quiet land now where the quiet sets itself and the lull sits in with us and mats down what could rustle so we convene in the quiet join and I open the hide bag and around me they've kneeled to the quiet I begin to undo the hide bag and bring out from in it the gall who's got milkstones and I have a fist of shells I array out in a market bend whose arc is a dusted tail and shells come out to lay there so they can see the cuts they could make and see the split of hide off the body with this and I delay for the banker's moment I'd seen it done in Spain to tell a story on what we traded and a delay the banker held to keep you from your own choosing so you could wait inside your wanting without a road to choose it was in that delay my homeland returned to me for a moment with its coins and clothing and tables and a single tongue and doors who tell a room from another and rows of something grown and a cistern in the square run from a spring we all used for its spring water one delay one bank-er's delay conjured it and then back again to the trading with the shells I had arrayed out like a fan or fishes tail dusted and it was an afternoon dusk and from then on I must have lied down in a sand hollow in night after we traded I cannot recollect followed back onto the island of Malhado where among them I found Oviedo and he is inside the hut on top of the oyster shells and his doctors are three Indian girls who graze his body in light touches they've seem to come to this as Oviedo has been unhealed and unwell this long time and still cannot rise from his

matted bed though the ministering is faithful he remains ill
or so I visit him inside his hut and the girl children continue
without me noticed I sit by to have his ear Oviedo my
Christian I will not leave without you I have found our
path to Pánuco I have wended down the way of Pánuco
and to know the way to there I have mapped it inside me
and it is written there well there is not a way it can be lost to
me there is no way it can become something else something
other than what it is which is our way to Pánuco I have
found us a way in the way of Pánuco and I will not leave
without you we must travel as one we must bring ourselves
from here and go along the coast and Oviedo laid there as
an ill man would lay and let out a weak cough and shuddered and his children doctors they tended him well
although I could tell his body was hale and his eye was hale
and clear and mended though it must have been a pantomime his illness for he said to me he was too ill to go and too
abominated to go with me along the coast and so I pled and
remapped our path along and still he pled sick and unable
and again and unfit to swim but I could not put myself to
have faith in this so I pled again that we must go the way of
Pánuco and I will do the swum parts that I have inside me
the map of us but Oviedo he would stay and continue his
sickness and continue his collection of the girls healing who
were there with him and so I left from there followed days
to know Oviedo was not in his person enough to go the
way of Pánuco and it would be another set of four seasons
until I could return to him with the case to leave and to
come beyond where we'd been as another hand to them but
Oviedo was not as moved as I was could this have been his
draw he might have guessed could this have been his end
where his own line on our maps ended could that have been
his sickness I brought this into the woods with me inland to

the trading sands where I laid out the shells and stones and
the ground roots the powder of whom had a value in its
look and in these I brought my unended thinking on
Oviedo and on trails inland I had Oviedo with me in thinking on the why and could it be a better plan and would our
Lord God look down upon us with kindness if we did stay
here and make this our land for him to blanket with his
grace and that grace itself unended could it be a better plan
I carried this and my sewn bags into and along the coast in
seasons and my body was itself its own vessel and its own
holder of a map so crossed and stars led me in night I slept
and took on the seasons followed in among the sodomites
who were there and they take the man to be a wife and this
man is passive and girlish and acts in all the ways in which a
woman does and stays inside the hut of bended reeds and
waits there for roots or for quiet I cannot in its entire be well
in knowing what is a reason for them the men wives of
them for why they wait and I blend among them my own
naked shape a shadow the same as any other man followed
days when the salted water and the dirt mixed in was
enough to get used to for the season was a cloud and a gather
with the bodies who'd upon trails I'd come up to and we'd
surround and again who was on the outside would trade
inward until it all swapped out again followed by the bleeding women who are to these Indians a poison whose vital
spell you wouldn't cross and what they touch then is poison
also for they gather only their own board and it is when the
women bleed when men become untrue and seek unholy
men another to join into the Lord God who made us all
would unmake us for the view of it so shipped and foreign
to the blessings he has with love handed down without
judge and pause here to watch a moth come in and go
slowly to the fire followed on the afternoon of the day by

the sun covered over as if the sun had set inside itself and set in the sky to hide its self it was covered over by what seemed its own shadow for what was left in day was a thin silver light and the birds kept from any sound but the Charruco stayed close to the ground and their women were hid and men fought single bouts with each other with sticks low to the sand to see who could be lowest in the silver light and soon the man was near buried and the sun back to full bright uncovered as it was and the women returned into the day followed by a stay I went against the seat of a nut tree and tended to the cuts on my footsoles the gouge white in fester and warm as such it lets off a deep white and red exit from a wounded mouth I could only have come by in a thousand tries I put on poultice to draw out the ponds within who seep and run out and my one foot is doubled of its size a twin who sits aside in compare and the swollen foot holds itself a wounded limb and I wait there shaded by the nut tree and without drink I wrapped the weep into the leaves who were the most near I could reach and night moons circled overhead and I have a coldness come over me of a make I know by now is a mortal coldness a chill who winds up with a man calmed into the ground I have my lean here against the nut tree and I could only ask our Lord God for sunlight to bend into where I was and as if it was sended down to me there inside the next morning a shade of sunlight came over me through a sky undrawn of any cloud and I did lean there with a chill taken and the sun up against it so to send it out to come to the victor of the two and I was the ground upon where the feud could hold itself and I the colden rake who until then have been guided by our Lord God and His fond hand and somehow spared the due ends of them who sailed in the outset and yet against a nut tree with chills and a double foot the sun and chill battled I sat leaned and was not done and when the sun rose farther and spread its heated shed on to me and for the unclouded shed it set down upon me and I willed it to burn off what ailed me I was a vessel for the shed it was and in two more days it was as if a hand had put its bless on my bigger foot to smallen it and I came up from the ground and moved my back backwards and sat down again against the nut tree but I knew then I was healed for now followed up into the Charruco and to where Oviedo was said to be and he did advance a case for why we shouldn't leave these Indians but this was the severalth time I came for Oviedo in the vernal month and there was no judge outside of ourselves this time and there were no fates who rode against us and if the hand of our Lord God did guide us and it did without question as it was beyond question so it was the hand of our Lord God shook us from there and Oviedo came with me and we left to go the way of Pánuco.

BEFORE THERE WAS A MAP THERE WERE TWELVE CHRISTIANS WHO LEFT CABEZA DE VACA WITH HIS ILLNESS AND WENT THE WAY OF PÁNUCO

Under the sun those years ago they setted along the coast toward Pánuco and the town of Pánuco there or so it might have been drawn to some of them. The coastal way was sanded, inleted, rivers who they must to cross run out from the inland plains. They traded bells and sable cloaks with Indians who crossed them over these waters in canoes and by swimming them across on their bodies and on bloated deer bodies who floated and there was a cord tied around the neck to cinch it.

There was a wide river who ran across their way and so they builded two rafts. Half the men on the first raft set across and they had their arms into the water meant to steer them and to get them to the far bank and this they did and stood up on ground over on the far bank.

The second raft was good until the meat of the river where the current was the most and drew them out to sea where they became small to the shore and two men swam back to shore and two men who were in a swim to shore came to the sea and died down underneath it and the one man left on the raft he stayed the raft and stood himself upright so that his body was jibbed and brought the raft with him back to shore by cause of the wind behind him.

THE DRIFT IS OVIEDO

In night we begin to Pánuco and Oviedo is with me in step but even in then I know he is not of our trek. We walk in sand together.

Side glances and his robe. He is in a dress for what I know of one. If he knows my eyes are turned he'll plot I can tell or he'll fashion an alter land for where he sets himself in night. Not enough he wouldn't rest with myself the night a wholly vagrant other we've unthought but Oviedo. I've dug us beds to be warm and Oviedo sets himself in crouch and his eyes are off to the past. His dress is gathered around him and around his neck for the warmer cuff of it.

I could look to when it was before we set our escape. Oviedo had a last talk with the Indian who shared his hut and this Indian was a man but he wore the same clothes as the women and he behaved as the women did and he did with his day what the women did and Oviedo was in close consult with this woman-man and in quiet I could not tell what they described to each other but they were both it seemed pulled apart on Oviedo leaving and the woman-man fell and cried and tore his basket and went underneath his own mat when Oviedo turned and left and we left there but I see Oviedo now with some of himself still back in his hut and with his woman-man.

Down leagues of coast toward Pánuco, the inlets and gaps in the coastline I swim with Oviedo on my back and side and he is like a field sack of wet grain who's in cling to me. We are both thin but we have a purpose now and so we walk thin but in stead.

We get across four rivers as such, Oviedo his grain sack on me and I can swim.

Some Indians from the near coast have come to us and they are called Deaguanes and they travel with us for two days and I have asked our Lord God if these men will do us harm or if these men are an agent of His guiding hand and I can not tell if the clouds who moved against the sun are a sign to me in either way. And so we follow each other in turn and walk our thin ways as one.

At the next crossing it is a wide river and deep and with a current who has a tall fist. I draw with my foot a symbol in the sand and this is a marker presented to his royal name whom God our Lord has willed to oversee our health and safe passage. On the shore of this wide river we halt as a thin band of us so haggard and without shevel and on the far bank some Indians have come and they cross the river in boats to see the Deaguanes who are with us. On the afternoon of this day these Indians tell us there are three men like ourselves farther on and they tell us their names and that the others have died of cold and hunger and the Indians farther on who hold the three men like us have killed three other of the Christians whom they name who were killed because they had drawn themselves across the ground in night so to guest themselves of no few homes and two others were killed on account of a dream that came to a child who saw in his slept vision the Christians allowing harm to seed out from them and so they were taken to the sand and thick wood brought down on them for an end. It was accounted how the three men like us who remained were treated with a foulness and to bring this to our senses these Indians rained down on me and on Oviedo a charge of actual blows by the hand and with sticks they had and they brought to our chests the points of arrows and sent a look from them of eyes set to harm us to the next and this went on so we could match our senses to how our fellow Christians lived. Oviedo on him was cut and damaged to blood as was I but Oviedo had a new flinch I can see in him and his eye has changed. He comes to me and his dress is gone badly and he tells me he can not continue for Pánuco there is only the same as these blows for us to come and beyond that nothing finer. From my load of why he shouldn't turn back there is not a line full enough to bring him with me. And so Oviedo, my companion, went back with some women of the Deaguanes and he turned from Pánuco and from me and he was away.

WITH THE QUEVENES

In the sand I am alone with the Indians who were called the Quevenes. They tell me the Indians who hold my Christian brothers will be at the tree of nuts in two days and we will go there. I go with them in their canoes across this wide river and on the far bank we stand up and then we walk and the sea is on our left and I am with these Quevenes and Oviedo gone.

Dim night come to the Quevenes and to me I've gone alone into the clutch of them. The swung stick and flown hand and mud thrown dement of them I cast them into an act inside the book I'm in to bring me to the outside of this where I can look down to me and witness my own sentence. The welts who now stand in for the lesson. I'm crabbed underneath a bough when night sets in and they've set off to heal each other without God.

My companion Oviedo he turned and went with the women of the Deaguanes and set himself a new pact to live howsoever into the ends of him. I can not put the tiles together so to make this exit. I can not even near the picture of it for me to blend back in with the trees and the nap of them to remain. What could have been built into him so that his current wend is so unseen by me? Is it not a testament to the grace of our Lord God that we so much as our sins would even allow the passage of us into the next we still in amble set us walking to Pánuco? But off he's gone and somehow this was a natural walk for him to take back to the roots and bramble and huts and so far back to the broken basket I must imagine he's on his way to from now until his ever.

In light I'm among the rabble and the gesture to move to not begin the day on fucked terms and come to gather wood and kill some thing or dig up some thing for all. We're in a run and wouldn't stop for what and we put a ring around the doe quarry and I see them there and one doe jumps up as if it wouldn't stop to rise away from us but then it fell and we advance and one doe breaks through our wall but the trapped ones stay and stillen themselves to hide in the broadness and we close down on them with our sticks and a rock inside a fist and bring them to our board skinned open and smoked. I have us in our hearts our Lord I have us to the ends of our hearts.

But most of what I come to you with our Lord God I come to you with an ever hope to be the vessel or to be the mirror or I can be the veldt who goes blown by the hint of your approach and I can go blown by the single wind you send across the ocean to us and I bend in the catch of you I lean down to full wash it over me.

And to the other three Christians we'll bring you they tell me and it is the faith in this who's the float to buoy me.

Headed to the banks of this wide river to the trees and to the nuts there. Another set of days to put my trust in the men who could end me and so I go along with the blindness I need to not turn back myself and to not lie down in the best sand to wait for my last night. I must be a man who walks. These Quevenes set upon the nut trees and the other men like me who will be there too or so. I know I am getting led. I'm on another's route and guided by the wind of them the near run they keep up as if they chase or as if they are pursued it must be a collection of the both.

In night the bodies of the men are impure and they move to one another as two shadows would and there is an animal sound I come to forgive and I forgive most all the acts and habits they posses but I swear there are lands across one can travel far enough from His grace too far to reach by any one mercy. I cover myself with the stars as they are there for me and then I wrap arms around my still able head and make a near dark room of it into which.

In a day a thick blow came in off the sea and we held up next to bigger trees who protected us from the wind who came in off the sea and so we waited huddled. Put ourselves into such small knots we could have been rock or almonds or the husk of an apple stone. We tied ourselves to the bottoms of the trees and held out until. The trees about the bottoms of whom they have abundant knees we clutch onto them. Are we not the sons of trees? All legs and arms and making shade when we can and water comes into us and we have our delicate parts up top where only the sun can put itself and feet dug in. Are we not the sons of almond and the sons of our home trees the nut elm and the leg oak we look back to the trees of our home and they are bark and knee and bowl and canopy and we fasten us to them here to so live throughout the blow. Even us, already blown by the fates and our very sins to the edges of the true good world here we are and stand good against the wind God sends across to us and we are good. We set stead and held to the trees – our fathers we're the sons of it seems at times I look up to the fixed canopy and the extend the branches have and I am in my father's bed with him an early thing I can recall and I am with him as in the branches above me held and set and for life a fixed arm I settle into, he's told me of the stars who pair up and descend and he's told me of the bulls who live inside the lawns of the moon and whose eyes are inside the wigs of elder women and how when I believed there was a demon in the topmost corner of my room he laid with me and we looked up together to the demon and he described it to me as if it was an ordinary, as if I was beholding an entirely else thing and together we unwrote the canvas held up there and demons fled with his explain I laid there in his crook and I could only have one desire then to unfound the demon there my father took and undid what I had done up there in the topmost corner.

Helded up by the bigger trees and hid next up to them for the lee side they give. Our sins again come out to be traded for and us naked again in sand blown through us. A shell tumbles on end and skids by like a boat and Miruelo is down there with his fucked maps and his fucked notions steering us all into his guess. When was that.

This night we collect us together and our things and a fire and the wind has gone past. We're rabble and one of my ears is wrong and padded. The night is through with us I can tell and fire only stays because it will.

Then we are on our way to meet the men who are the other Christians I can only guess of whom and if at all they are on this land by the grace of our Lord God their sins somehow equal to mine and we've been spared the weather the rest of them have come up against.

I am led to a briar where we can see the grove of nut trees and by hands I'm told to stand down and hide there so our undetect is full. And in the end of a life must it be so? The spot I'm in fully built by another man whose cross with your own life was up until then unguessed. The end times we feel by the way the world moves on without us, our agency nulled out by the grander paths man is up to. The end times spelled out in the sure which is a walk we join in on for some of it but then it goes on ahead while we think on our own demise and how it could have come to this, that moment we all guess is unknowable and so we send it off as if it's a day who never comes. In a crouch with the Quevenes and in a moment I can feel the rock-head come down on me and with my head stove in I welcome what I could never have seen until then.

So waiting in a moment when the flesh of us is weighed against the offer of a floated milkweed pod there is a bird who sends her call. Common and usually flit. Branching up there from one to another and her call is common also, just a breedle in the mix of all that's heard.

How must our Lord God deem upon us our maps so unknown to us and so known to Him. Our paths who cross another man's path. The rivers and the wind who runs between the woods. How must our Lord God weigh our purpose so to save us for some great upcoming. Or for some furtherance in the crossing of the map of another man.

Hidden here now inside my purpose alone and with the Indians who guide me. Hid here behind a bramble and the nut trees waiting. They motion to me to say that this is where the Christian comes and they are sure and nod sternly about the truth of it. To here from the huts who gather past the nut trees.

Later in the day it was Andrés Dorantes as a man himself came to the nut trees from the far huts and was close by to where I was hidden. I saw him there but then my astonish at seeing him told my eyes that he was not there. It was not Andrés Dorantes because it could not be. And then my body knew it was not him so that I backed away from the bramble there who hid me and my Indians although they meant to keep themselves hidden also they held me to my stand. Stilled again I trembled there and I could not look out to what was beyond our hide. It was my body already in decide but these Indians held me there. They must have known that I had seen an alter man, a living different spirit man who I could not trust or believe and so they held me there to allow the ghosting. Then a near bird sounded. A breeze moved the limbs in front of me. The bird again sounded. Then Andrés Dorantes was there again among the nut trees.

When Andrés Dorantes was near to me I came out from behind the bramble and we saw each other there with a clearing between us who became smaller and we embraced with our hearts against each other's and we wept for the astonish in us both and for the time when it was thought the other man had met some true end and for the wisdom of our Lord God to set our maps down of us to cross and to be us here and then.

It was deemed that I had been held alive and it served our Lord God to maintain me to the life and to continue us who remained for all the sickness and sea and hardship and the brutal hands laid on me our Lord God was then served to hold my walk up to the sun so that it would grow and continue and so I continue and it was deemed that my delivery to Andrés Dorantes and his slave Estevanico and then to Alonso del Castillo was the true banner it was the bell who announced that it was time to become uncaptive of the Quevenes and to go the way of Pánuco. So that I might carry them on my body through the swum parts of where it was we headed. So that our new charts were drawn and decided.

Of the Indians there at the nut trees I was given to the Indians who held Castillo. The foremost among them was blind in one eye and the wife of him was blind in one eye and there was a son of them who was blind in one eye and the man nearby them it was not told what he shared with them and he was blind in one eye and these Indians were called the Marianes.

As Castillo knew the habits of these Marianes and what the brutal of them could be and how they valued a captive and what their travel routes would be for the seasons we builded a plan to run from them when the Marianes brought us to the land of the prickly pears and there we could join again Dorantes and Estevanico and go the four of us away and to Pánuco.

In nights the mosquitoes set upon us and to set up something against them the Indians built fires in a ring around us all and put onto the fires wet logs who instead of burning let off smoke in thick yards who burned our eyes so that we could weep of it. To get out from inside the smoke and to chase some dear rest we went to the shore to sleep on sand until we were found by an Indian who clubbed us back into the smoke and to the unmissing and ungone.

They eat the skins and tails of lizards and ants and ant eggs and a snail they trick onto wooden plates and the shit they find is eaten and the bones of fish and deer and deer hoof is dried and ground into a dust and made into a paste and this is eaten.

We see a brutal half-year when it seemed our Lord God had turned away from us and then our Indians are setting to the prickly pears and we as Christians in our sin and owing still for the unnumbered sins we must have laid by it is the time for the escape we've come up with. Dorantes and Estevanico are there as captives and in secret I tell them of the plan to leave. Then the moment of enacting it has ended its approach and so we arrange a final cleave but on the verge of us in exit the Indians our captors come to wild blows and branches swung to hit and deep hacks into the top were brought down it was a test of mad bodies and it was caused by a woman too young to be a proper wife and bloodied in the mix our captors each defeated took us into separate ways so that I was alone with Indians and Castillo was alone as well as Dorantes and Estevanico so that we could not speak in any way and it was then we knew we couldn't have a chance to leave until we all returned to the land of the prickly pear the next year.

So our Lord God gave to me another year and so it served
Him to protect me from an end and wove for me a terrible
home with them my captors who went foodless often and
saw to my sentence in brutal sides.

Preserved and protected by our Lord God to continue in a path who aimed at settling our debts against the sins we carried and I was preserved until the next year and when the Indians my captors returned to the land of the prickly pears and Castillo and Dorantes and his slave Estevanico all returned by the hand of our Lord God we agreed to escape that night but in the day we were again divided and this was a cancel to the plan. But before our divide I set down an offer to my Christian brothers that I would wait for them in the land of the prickly pears until the moon was full and if the moon was full and they have not yet come I would go the way of Pánuco alone and without them.

Counting moon days and they lay on me like a coat would. My count is added to at dusk and she brings herself up as only a thin edge as brief as she could be and lit yet an arc her lash cresting. One. Upcoming us to the common count. The building of her over days she mounts an expand who dusk rises and she leaves dusk to rather night and hold risen.

Waking she's above and held there and waking again she's over some and waking again she's put her shining back onto clouds who walk between us.

And they come, Dorantes and Estevanico. On the thirteenth day of our moon so it was near full and gave us all in night a full view of what grew there and they approached me in that view given down by the wide moon and they came next to me in naked walk so the wide moon put a new sick gaunt to them and had their faces drawn and their beards so knotted not a man could fix the tangles ever but they came next to me.

For Castillo I'm come to this – Castillo was held and fastened to him was a sail who drifted him above the boiling sins he's done and who remain as sins who wait for when he's paid for them but until then remain on grand ledgers so our Lord God the protector ties upon him the sail of His deliverance who uplifts Castillo up over his entire boil and sets him down with us so that at once we are again the four of us and drafting into plans our next upcoming.

We come now to be the man who has become a silken pip. Flown outside the pod and gustblown the four men each an own germ. So four Christian men led only by the grace of our Lord God as if ordered by tides to be sent through channels where deep sea runs we go sent by His grace to be the floated seeds He intends and to be the silken.

It is only to accept this and we do at once to be in His love.

We go us now us four in thin shamble with the sea out on our left and also where the sun rises and we go us in the way of Pánuco.

In nights we join up close and huddle like dogs to sleep with the heat who ran out from the one who was under.

Walking in day ahead two vines rise made up of smoke. We go on and send Estevanico up ahead to speak with a sole Indian who's been overtaken by us. The Indian leads us on and by the vespers hour we come to the camp and huts of these Indians who have just setted up here this day.

These Indians had tunas the fruit flowers of the prickly pear abundant and they presented to us the tunas on account of our Lord God and his healing they all knew we'd let to them these Indians who were called the Avavares. This our Lord God the same who kept alive the four of us to now through so much desolate of it and put a people in our path to cross who could with open hearts not enharm us but instead give us a bowl and each a mat for us each to be on.

God's mapmaking becomes known to us. We step into the lines drawn by our Lord God his wide parchment unscrolled to better guide us on longer routes and we tread them so we tread them unguessed of any alter route or path. Guided and beyond kemp though polished in our belief and trust or so. Dorantes and Castillo and Estevanico we then go along threads pulled out by our Lord God and I do well to believe I do well to know the route is well. Ambled south on our purpose to Pánuco and I do not let from me the notion that our map is anything but His sended alone.

The day is held to long study. Ambled in a mostly unsaid walk it is a quiet progress. The sanded lowlands we cross and there is no path but only a way forward until a clearing or until the sea is heard to the left of us. Some bug unfortunate in its own path to be in our way is hunted quickly without comment and pressed down and had. As a lizard or an already dead bird not rank enough to bury it's also had sometimes shared in a pulling apart. The sometime wind to shore who on days when it could appease it was a gusted bend in what the common draft was upon us.

Continued us and to the next. Guided by whom would lead us and there was a myth of us among the Indians that we could heal and bring luck or the reverse of that and so we should be treated well and all possessions should be given to the guiding Indians who brought these men. Arriving to a new camp meant the welcome of us and the sacking of their possessions by our guides who returned loaded down with more than they could carry and we were then to be with these new Indians who then guided us to the next. Our travelling group a growing crowd and hundreds came with us and we could not remove us from them and we continued.

Sanded us and our steps follow one and then another. Ahead is Estevanico as a hued guide his gaze ahead and somewhat upheld as if in the bowls of the trees we come under have a better clue to lend and he can see it there inside the crossing shade as if in the patterns of the leaves there appeared to him some Moorish tapestry out of which he pulls a thread who unravels and the path of that unravel puts a map down on his table inside and unscrolls it. Estevanico sold to Andrés Dorantes de Carranza and sailed to New Spain and with us to Florida and then at some time became no longer of Dorantes but instead of Estevanico the man of himself unowned it seemed and of his own accord in now an amble with us and hued he ambles with us ahead at times and now ahead and himself a guide with us behind him but instead it could be himself a lead for him alone into the abundant upcoming into which he guides himself as his own account is taken down by the sun and clouds and in consult with his steps he sees in the lattice of branch and leaf the builded charts who limn us and our way. He's now the guide who guides us and we follow for the unchoosing in it and we follow into the upcoming in the belief that our belief is undead our belief is continued and will continue with him up ahead.

The leaves and bowls above the same to us all and how it is below for us all under the maze of it. But is it each his own read of what's above?

Dorantes up ahead. He who sleeps upside-down.

Dorantes and when he isn't sleeping he is walking. In night the sun is gone it's past dusk into the night we've pulled up branches and dried fallen fronds dug motes in dirt for us as bodies to lie into for the walls it lifts around us and the cool of it so we've all set us up and Dorantes in night is a man who walks instead out to a near copse to bend in his hand the bark or pull off buds who would have served any Indian behind us instead undressed to the floor to lie Dorantes in night he's wandered on to the bend we up until then have come upon and Dorantes is there upon the bend and we are slept but Dorantes has himself into the bend and wet he's in a waded pause it seems from the piece of him I can see of him he's waded at the bend and then landed again to walk in night the bramble we've stepped aside of and Dorantes is in among it full step and him his own guide a thorn wouldn't lag him he's in his night walk no matter. See the moon the woman of the sun and it is us underneath her good embers who rest and when Dorantes is in his wander we see him there returning to us from his night walk and he returns as if it was no other and he lies down in dirt with us to rest and we sleep although in night it is still not sleep as we've know it to be.

Alonso del Castillo Maldonado he's up and gone ahead of us and we're in tatters come to follow for the following is a chooseless abide. What he's done is up ahead and he's gone there his body one ship he's an ear to and us in tow and Castillo he's a man on parchment with a number and a ledger all columned set he's up there defaulted to the lead and commanding of himself a version of the utmost and us in tow we've assigned us to the Indians them all who follow for now and he's cutted bramble he's cut aside deep olden cypress knees in cuts impossible to enfathom he's swung aside and a path of us he's cut man-wide of us to line us up through behind him enough for us all to go through.

The frond of him ahead, casted to us as a cairn left to us in a shadow, us shaded and queued on a sanded graph, him ahead added to the ledger us all true, come us and all.

Following Castillo. He's gone and cut the ferns I've picked out ahead of us to serve as a waypoint and then he's gone to truly hack them down low.

WE BEGAN TO SEE MOUNTAINS

We began to see them who rose up leagues into the sky in unbroken heave out from the sea.

We began to see a line of mountains who up from out of the sea were becoming to rise in upwards described to us as enormous.

We began to see mountains who rose up from the sea on our left and looking to the south the mountains continued to our right in an unbroken list of ridges and peaks who started at the sea and went along in continuous gathering upward unbroken.

We began to see ahead of us at a distance which almost undid our belief in what the tallness of them could be as how our eyes could false up a thing in time was an ever caution so we in our own study began to see them rise there like a ghost far off who you could wish to come apart and go back into itself and be gone before a word about it would come up of it but instead the ghost is become more shapen with a ridge and with a shadow who lays into the walls of rises with dark ravine cuts until at once among the waited moments we untold each other it became sure they were such tall mountains who grew up from the sea and went inland to break up what plain was there and to continue off into where the sun sets to that place beyond our seeing.

We began to see the cut down near the sea where the mountains met the sea and there we were told by our guides that the men who lived there in that cut of hillside and sea were always at war and to pass through there meant to not continue past and our guides would not go with us to the cut and so we turned us inland at a wide river who ran there toward the hills.

V

The hills are bigger than the hills, bended down from out of where they come, stacked and sided and running down from the whiter sky who moves above them evenly and mutely in a steady unwatching whiteness tumbled across that firmament through which it descends in a good slope from up in those peaks descended down in foothills a continuous drop at an angle to the foothills who describe that joining of the hill and of the valley floor like an ankle to the leg fell down from clouds and tapered into the foot. It is here the men and women set rested and splayed from the mouth of the river at the sea and clouded up the edges of the river arranged some by family some by sets of women who dug roots and washed them in the river some by men who fought and the men and boys who crowded near to shout in upon it here they all banded.

The crowd of them are returning along the route they arrived on, filing back along the river valley and at a pace of one who returns and knows what comes ahead. In time the men who remain there alone on the bank of the river are only Cabeza de Vaca and Castillo and Estevanico and Dorantes and it is the Indians who return. The four men do not know why the Indians will not join them for the journey inland and upriver. Could they see only desolation ahead or were there known threats? Had they gone far enough from where they'd always been? It is in the afternoon. The river has a light sound and the sun is on them at an angle and unbroken by any cloud.

The four men walk upriver among a thicket who in a passive way opposes them. They move unaccompanied save by each other. The ground they go on scrubbish and rocked, the bellies of their feet worn hard and cured like something taken from the sea and dried in the sun. Come up above and see the four men alone walking haggard and steady and silent to the next and of a pace who mentions no rush and also no lag into the day when the sun crosses to dusk. This is the last time the four will travel alone, unaccompanied, and they move ahead in silence and with an unsaid purpose.

Inside this tall light the four men come to a setted grove where two dozen grass and reed homes stand in no plan or fixed arrange. When they are seen to arrive there is a general sadness and weeping overcomes the men and women of this setted grove and they have been told what becomes a place when the four men arrive and they fall to weeping and they put their hands into their hair and they pull at the hair they hold on to and lift up their arms to look upward and for it all the weeping is upon them. But then it is clear that the four men have arrived as only four men and without a guiding band who would demand their only items. The weeping ended and the four men were given prickly pear and nothing else. Evening came and the four men were near each other in sleep on the ground and there was the sound of night bugs who clicked and rattled and there was a piece of light from the moon who stood down to them in sleep and there was the sound of the night when there is no day left in it.

In the new day when there is still them all asleep there is a return of the Indians who had gone back down the river the day before. They set upon the sleeping grove and sack it to the bone and haul off beyond what they can all command so again there is a weeping. It is told to the Indians of the grove that the four men were sended down from the sky and the four men can heal or bewilder or kill or set sickness upon at will and these four men should be handled well unless they will bring cause upon them. The Indians of the grove speak among themselves and then their lord presents to the four men his palms held out and held upward and his head bowed lightly. There is a general deference and an exceeding acknowledgement of the four men and there is drawn around them an unseen circle where the sanctity of the four men is maintained.

As such these Indians and the four men who remained from the Narváez expedition continue on into the mainland following upstream a wide river and the number of them all put up a dust about them and a general commote and so it is for three days of travel of them all. Led or accompanied it isn't sure. It is a chaos of them all in transit to the next.

The Indians ahead come to a village of forty huts first and they bring news to the village that they are among men who have come down from the sky these men who have the power to heal and to unheal and of powers even beyond these who become more builded up with each retelling as if to outlandish even themselves in the telling. In this setted stage the four men come into the village and the great rejoicing at their arrival commences and reverence is at hand upon them. Two physicians from the village present to each of the four men a gourd in which there is some water and it is noticed that only the village elders and physicians have an own gourd and that a gourd itself is what can set apart one man from others.

Travelling inland and upriver they send Estevanico into the open unaccounted space between the three of them and the most of the others. In this way it is Estevanico who transacts with an exchange of common gestures and acquired sounds who stand for things or ways, Estevanico among the Indians and the three Spaniards removed in counsel away from the negotiates. The three shaded and set off from the trading and the mapping and them who ask to have their sickness brought away and them who have one enormous limb or skinned leg to solve.

They head inland with those gourds to announce the station of the four and with them their shepherd Indians who guide them to the next place to sack and carry off more than what they can haul with them and leave most of what was hoisted casted off. Rugs and mats and animal skins and hides and stones that had been reshaped and reeds woven into a brittle fabric all carried off until it was then left again casted off in the order of its trivia. Left to be under the bird sounds and the clicking of the bugs who are there but unseen and left until the ones who are just sacked to come later up that same route and gather again what is theirs to then be theirs again.

Gourds who floated down the river after coming undone these calabazas from an upstream only guessed, grown dark or suncolored and then dried down the rounded husk who then is blown or somehow left teetered on the banks above this river and then fallen so to float them turning and atop the small riffs then to move by some design to where.

Gone upstream by as well some design they engather in a movement at once directed and then also wandered set to a general way. Eighty leagues into the inland in this assume. Sacking what possibles are come across and leaving shambles. Estevanico as a gourded agent of the gourded men, distant healers sent from the upper sun and now surrounded. Eighty leagues the manner of whom scripted above and to the inland they maunder.

Forty houses well inland they all come to, arriving amok in an afternoon long undrawn and much like those who were earlier as a dusk becomes upon them all the forty houses and them all in arrival upon them. With the introduction is a gift among the many this one handed to Andrés Dorantes who is given a copper bell and on the bell is a face in the image of a person as if drawn in the sand by a child and the copper bell is thick with itself and is the size of a paroquet and it is cast.

In among the Indians of the forty houses is at least a cotton shift who woven and dyed deep red is indeed a loomed thing and of a nearfound cotton so it is agreed to be important to the four as with the bell in that each is a note from some larger opus who must be adjacent or so.

A woven and dyed shift of woven cotton as a marker for the land upcoming. Dorantes and a bell made of copper cast into the opposite of the shape of the true bell. Dorantes and his new bell an object who as well is a marker for an elsewhere in where a copper bell is cast or also where cotton becomes a thread into a woven cloth and then into a deep red shift an elsewhere it must be not all too distant an elsewhere of a people who could build these markers and enough of them to trade or send away. Estevanico as the agent of the four and with an astonish about him what of his astonish he is unable to hide from coming to view Estevanico as the agent of the four he motions for a council with those Indians who seem to hold themselves more upright and wear a gaze who is in return of the eyes set upon them Estevanico goes to them in council. Then it is said in gestures and in sounds who draw a picture it is told these bells and cotton shifts come from a land to the north in that direction and in that land to the north there is much more of it all and of the copper and the cloth there is a notion that these things have tall value among them.

They set off at dawn and go to the north, some of them of the Indians who left the forty houses to go north with them and some from earlier and more downstream who among them all are guides and then there are the Indians who still join the march as in an old tale handed down about the men who came from the heavens and how it was to follow them and they were themselves a role in that old epic. The land they cross is itself as if a rod had been dragged across the sand and then it rested there dark and languid under the sun they all cross under and the land they cross is seven leagues for all of them it is the day entire and for some it is more yet. When there is an evening they come to where some houses are set along the treed banks of a slow bend in the river there and who live there come out from those houses and toward the array of them in travel. There are children on the backs of the men and women and some wear skins of hide when others wear a similar cotton to the deep red shift and there is a shining drawn onto their faces in circles around their eyes so that there is a ring of shining silver like halos two on each face who approach to welcome in a way. It is already known that who arrive are men who can summon the power of the wind and who can with a brief will cast out an illness or settle the disputes of other men. Bags of silver and meat hides and beads hard as stones and polished all of this is given to the arrivals and this all is handed to those who followed and then so divvied.

In day a man is brought to the four and inside him is an arrowhead who came in by the front of his shoulder and passed down towards his heart and he lived in only great pain. He is brought to Cabeza de Vaca and Cabeza de Vaca puts his hands upon the Indian. He can push on the Indian and he can hear with his fingers where the arrowhead remains and it is stiff gone wedded into something rigid and meant. With a knife Cabeza de Vaca cuts into him and he is stern but his eye wanders up into the canopy and the knife goes in to reach to where. The point of the knife hits the arrowhead and clicks off to the side and the Indian with his head gives a twitch as if there is no way to be unmoved by this passage into him and the blade is bladed in to better ken the edges of the intrude and it is full lodged at that. It could be the Lord God of a hand in this. It is a delicate plan to be about. Into the Indian the knifehead goes edging and finds his ail the bone of this arrowhead set tight against his gristle who holds him fast and to pay him with so many edgings of the blade dug in to so pry his lodge and click it up and click up and out from in him and it is tweezed out with two knives. When the arrowhead is out they all huddle and ask to see and have the arrowhead and they take it and display it up to them as if the sun had to do with it. The Indian is bleeding from this and it runs down the front of him in small gouts so Cabeza de Vaca takes a stitch into the skin with the blade edge and with a fiber to pass it through into the skin and takes another stitch in him to solve the bleeding. Upon this Cabeza de Vaca lays what was scraped of some hide who is by and the tallow it shod is laid on waxish on the wound. So until the morning when the stitch and other stitch is pulled out and the Indian puts his arm above him and tells them all of the ruined tells he had from all the pain he spent and could they all wait to settle in for this his own renewal and he comes into the day without the olden gripes he had and he is then or so among the well. And then his scar is nothing more than a palm line from then on.

Then it is the bell brought out and it is asked again where this bell is from. And them who'd seen the arrowhead come again from inside a cousin they all put a blanket on the bell and describe how these are abundant at the place where the houses do not move.

They set out in that direction in the soonest morning. The new Indians carrying clubs who are as long as their own legs. The Indians going about their travel in paths as if they are in line two lines in a marching step.

Ahead of them are the Indians who carry huge clubs and beat the game they come across. As a hare shows itself from under sage and begins its dart out from there these Indians who carry huge clubs run up and around the hare to surround it and to swing down upon the hare with those clubs. The clubbing draws in to the small quarry and the hare unable to figure on the route to save itself darts up and directly into the arms of an Indian berserk with hunger and the chase and the Indian with a hand on a foreleg and the other hand gripped around the neck of the hare pulls it apart to make two hares and both of them at rest.

There were Indians who fan out and go not in groups but alone and without sound but with a purpose and a steady gait and what they seek ahead of them with arrows and bows are deer and antelope. These Indians do not go ahead but instead are like the haze who in the morning is near the far edges of the camp and then in sun is gone but comes to return again in the evening. For these hunters it is determined and they are taller in the evening. Hauling into camp the several deer and quail who are stripped of their outsides and rendered for what of it can be used or eaten which is near all.

It is told in camp about the bird who the Indians would not club or kill or aim an arrow at. In a pantomime an Indian raises his arms out sideways and flaps them slowly and holds them out while he himself lopes in an almost hopping lope with his feet in near time and he has painted his face and neck the color red of some fruit there was a pile of. Loping in this way they tell in camp how the buzzard is not to be taken from its place for how it looks to be an ancient man and how it circles overhead to protect them and to guide them along the best routes. As if the circles they describe overhead are the halos Cabeza de Vaca had seen on church frescoes. The elder protectors above.

In evening the ovens so called are dug and fired and all the game is altered into meat and parted out and laid into the oven without ceremony. Deer heads and legs are laid in alongside whole quail and headless jackrabbits and there is a lizard put in by an Indian boy and skulls of antelope with the spiral horns clubbed off and those horns in turn put to use. The bigger skins set aside for something else. It all a profane ritual for some end who is invited to come quickly.

There are some nights in camp when over some thousands are about and they are all about some way to bring about the next meal. When this meal is ready and the ovens are opened and deer legs pulled up from out of it smoking and wet it is the custom to have each Indian's meal blessed by the holy men from the sky and it is the sign of the cross or a breath blown down upon a charred quail. The thousands of them all in line and each unable to eat until it has been blessed by the four men into the night the sign of the cross or a breath blown down upon a burned hock.

Much of them in line to do so for the chance to become close to one of the four men who blessed. To come up to one of those full beards who sit not so much among the dust and dirt but instead seem to be above the ground by what could be but only one small piece of air.

In night the meal entirely pulled apart and bones hucked off to the side and hauled into the darkness for those olden men to stand wingspread and boil over the next day.

228

They all continue in the direction of what is believed to be where the copper bell is from or to where it is the copper bell was made in some way it is the copper bell who tells the Indians where to lead them all. It is in this way that the guiding hand of the Lord conducts them in the form of a copper bell, the bell itself sent down from the heavens it seems and the bell understood by all ears and who beheld it. When a new Indian people are encountered and met and after they have offered everything they have and those things are divvied out by the Indian lords who travel with them and these new dispossessed fall in with the enormous company made up of the four Narváez survivors and the thousands of Indians from lord to hunter to handler to elder and infant it is related to the new followers that by the guidance of the copper bell it will be known in what direction they all continue.

They cross a wide river who runs with a depth and it flows from the north. The hunters up ahead first test the crossing with their clubs and antlers held above them and the river coming up to near chest high. Some lords cross the river bodily and unattended as a pronouncement and other lords are carried across the river on shoulders or on quickly builded litters of tree branches and reeds and this is also a pronouncement.

Beyond this there are the high plains over which they travel for two weeks. Coming to greet them then are other Indians who come from far away and they too give everything they have to the four men which in turn is divvied up by the Indian lords who travel with them. The copper bell is held up and described to the new followers and how it is a guide for them all and so it is agreed.

They cross a vast deserted stretch where it is dry and the mountains there are difficult to cross and rugged and there are days when only a few leagues are traveled for the hardship and for the hunger. There is no game there. The hunters when they set off do so at dawn and return in early evening at a loss for what. Scrub roots are dug up and tested and anything edible is first presented to the four Narváez survivors. There is great hunger among them all and each day the olden or broken of them are left to remain in some nearly shaded grotto and that will be their final place. For more than four weeks they travel through this dryness and the shambling company diminishes and many fall ill from hunger but the circling buzzards overhead give them hope and a more open eye. In evenings there is only a mat for the handlers to set down and no branches or trees and the handlers post watch as if petals all facing outward and sleep on their haunches.

They arrive at a river who is far to cross and runs at depths up to the shoulders of the tallest of them and it runs in a steady breathing time and it is a day for them all to cross and some of them to cross again so returning again to the side where the ones who can not cross alone wait. On the far shore some wait inside the water sitting and drinking or looking down into the passing rills as if there might be some answer to build out of the procession or else as if the sum of the unknown was held there and displayed again each moment to the following moment the river itself an endless and sourceless body laid down here in the bottom of the land or they wait inside the water to be cool and it has been many leagues from when there was a river to wait inside.

Woven mats of reeds who were pulled up in mudded flats near the bends in rivers laid down in lines and woven as such through unders and overs the ended pieces tucked under. Clubs as long as their own legs to club down game as small as voles the club worked at in the downtime with a found flint a sharpened edge dealt into the clubhandle in a scribbled maze the pattern took apart and mapped could only be the inner maps of who was carving or it could not. Gourds and arrows sended down from what wood makes a good shaft and what rock or polished stone on the flatlands of the caldera makes a worthy cutting head and band with a builded twine who's been coiled around an ankle for weeks.

They go bended broken to the sierra flattening. Met there by a people from away who come to witness the four healers and to bestow what they have. They bring piñon nuts from away and these they bestow.

To the witness it is noted the four ask to go to where the sun sets. The witness sees the mood and quiet huddle of the people from away who say that from here to where the sun sets it is a blank land and the nearest people more than far.

To the witness it is seen the four men in anger and demanding and it is seen then the three women of the people from away begin to walk in the direction where the sun sets and they are sent from there as scouts to learn what comes ahead.

The women who leave to scout come to a fate of their own. Ahead in foothill canyons and washes, cuts who went yellow and red if there had been water run through them. Across the hardened talc of dry creeks who had been always dry for what they knew of them. Up to a rise in gradual lift the women climb into cooler nights among the scrub and brittle trees no taller than the women at all and in night they keep to each other closely for the heat each other has.

On a night when there was little moon the women who were close they all put at least an eye up to the vault above them and the holes in the fabric. And they all see the sudden tear in that fabric pass from one end so across to reach the line where the mountains drew their own shadow against the blackness and one of the women hides her eyes for what she believes is upcoming when a thing is torn above you and one of the women comes undone by the sight of it and does not allow them to rest but to walk instead some yards ahead for the omen who lives in that moment they were in. And as it is told the woman who did not hide her eyes and did not come undone is the remaining woman and she is the youngest of them and it is known that when she was born she was given a thing to live by and it is unsure if it was a gift or if it was not a gift how she could know the language in full of another people from one day in sit with them and it was her who put a basket together to catch birds in and it seemed there was an older man who lived inside of her and so she was sent off to walk in peril no few times and returned again as if there was no peril she brought herself through it is told this woman did not hide or come undone but is able instead to note the shift in color of this event from the color of the sun in brief and then the moon and then a gem green is the light who lights up the bench of where they are.

235

It is told the youngest of the scouts was often sent on errands who would have kept any man among them down and it was always she who returned well and it was not told if she was sent out for the habit of hers to be well and return or if there was some other purpose. In among her people when she as a scout returned she was half welcome and none of them are of a skill to make a secret of their intention it is all worn on the outside of them.

Five days later the scouts return. The three women say it is a passable route up along the foothills inland with its own brand of what the days would fold to them but it is a route without a people within it. Not another set of whom for days. It isn't known how far ahead it is for them to come upon some other.

On the word of them they sleep to decide when the nexted day became. What dream could visit lend a hand in this decode? Fitless rest has all of the four men that night. Night visions of any use it was none. Some rambling of another time all joined up with the sea and when rafts held them to the sea it was when a fresh water gourd was golden and them in drift the sea a risen field with its own fated mood it was all unsure.

Huddled there in decision and low tones. But the next refuge on the way to where the sun sets is too far and the Indians drift from their huddle and become without aim and without a cure for the path ahead.

This refusal causes weather in the health where men and women become ill and grow false to themselves and writhe on shaded mats enfouled of themselves their bodies weak but mustering a quiver and then a death rattle until death overcomes and so eight of them are come to this end.

Hands are thrown up and scalps beaten by the owners of them and a circle stomping to the cloud healer and the moon healer to all this no avail. The sickness unimpeded at wit's end of them sets in for they are only certain that they've crossed the four men and this is what has come of it.

Sickness so the fever comes around the fallen like a bell woven in place from the shoulders beginning down from there in a chill and the head is light enough to pend aft and the eyes with only sky to measure turn upward to the math of the clouds and sea between them down from there into the cave where the heart is hung to smolder and push notes up into the hearing and the cave where the heart is hung an empty skid about who the woven chill is a keg and down from there is only trembled unassigned limbs adrift and unset in essence gone and left to become undone without guidance from above become extras to the body up above become the trembled gates unmanned. Shit puddles in the trough one trough dug for each fallen ill covered again with the soil dug out so each ill body rested there with legs hidden under soil and what's above soil in the bell of fever.

Huddled in decision and true fright. The sick are left to stay and the well continue with the four men upriver. On farther scouts and messengers sent ahead they now return to tell that ahead there are very few people for they have all set off to pursue the bison and only the olden or incapable remain.

After three days the assembled in travel stop and a camp or so is arranged. Scouts again set off with now Castillo and Estevanico.

They follow near the low lands where the river draws a wide line and the scouts bring them to a place where another river who comes down from out of mountains who stand up from where. One of the scouts who is a captive of the other scout she tells them that ahead into the mountains and upriver is the village of her people and where her father lives. They continue into the mountains and upriver.

To Castillo and Estevanico the village upriver and into the mountains when they arrive is at first unbelieved. The houses here seem fixed as if the people here do not leave or carry their houses on their backs to drop them where the next food is come across. For three days Castillo and Estevanico come to learn about this village and they witness the planted squash and frijoles and the maize plotted various and many.

Returning to the camp where Dorantes and Cabeza de Vaca wait this is all recounted and as a body is moved when dire becomes something other so true thanks is sended to Lord God for this grace upon them.

Where two rivers meet to become one. Two lines on a map one drawn in the flood plain one drawn with sudden shifts and turns so hard angles come about two lines drawn down to a low point to become one line.

Who were they to plant a calabash and mats of frijole and to send up maize from the nearby ground and to build a house who wouldn't drift off. Who were they to blanket and robe the skins drawn off by dark stones scaled to knifishness of the bison taken down by the many by augur and pike and arrow. Who were they to hold as uncontested that to reach the next village where maize was tended there would be seventeen days of eating only a dusted seed pod and then another seventeen days before reaching the people of the maize.

They follow this course laid out and guided by a renewed cast upon each village landed. Days spent famished and stumbled, a hoarded ball of deer fat the chiefest thing between them and a starved end. In each village arrived they find the people in their houses with their all belongings in the middle of the floor and each member of the house sits facing outward and their black hair left to fall in front of their faces like black oiled veils. Days and weeks of a starved amble over land beyond uncharted. Upon a people who ate powdered grass and this was a sign from Lord God to build hope and continue. Until it was true they came upon first a member and then the people of the maize.

The people of the maize have fixed houses and worn paths between houses and the houses where the maize is stored and rows of calabash and frijole. There are cactus nearby and two women each using a deer tail for a brush do brush from off the pads small bugs the cochineal who shade those pads and brush them off onto wooden boards cupped for doing this and they mound them.

To an astonish there were long mantles of woven cotton and these were dyed deep red and this is observed by the hearts of the four men and it is enough to lift them to a risen mood.

From the house of maize they go accompanied to the setted sun for more than a hundred leagues of desert and river valley. In the villages one more west than the one before the villages have fixed houses some of mud and some of an armature of branches bended covered in reed mats, houses for the storage of maize and calabash in rows and frijoles dried and stored. In the villages the four men are given deer hides and mantles of cotton and cotton robes the cotton finer than the mantles of New Spain and they are given beads and coral and turquoise that comes from the north and Dorantes is given several arrowheads made of emerald and these also come from the north in trade for plumes and the colored feathers of parrots. The women in the villages wear cotton shirts who come down to the knees open in the front and the women wear buckskin covers on their feet and on these leagues heading westward it is so. Between the villages on the routes they travel it does occur that a child is born from one among them all and each new child is brought to the four men so the child can be blessed and touched by these men from the sky and in each new village all members come to be blessed by the four men and for the multitudes to be blessed this is enormous and often is the occupation of a day. And the four men are always accompanied along these leagues leading westward as a new people are encountered the guiding Indians with a ceremony and a consultation of the elders relinquish their guide and hand over the four men to the people of the next village. The leagues of uncharted and chartlessness. A village where Dorantes is given six hundred deer hearts cut and dried or cured and this village is named by the four men Corazones for the hearts there and Corazones is itself an entrance to the many lands who border on the South Sea.

Keeping to the tended lands just inland from the South Sea they continue southward until there is a river who becomes too swollen from a week of rain to cross and then another week of rain and this entire movement is halted in a mudded camp. Days to bless and rest and to make the sign of the cross and touch the ill and the well alike. Inside the rain sitted under reed mats hung over bended poles Castillo watches an Indian pull heated rocks from a fire and drop the rocks into a gourd half filled with water and some frijoles and Castillo sees around the Indian's neck a cotton cord and on the cord is the buckle from a belt used to keep a sword and sewn into the cord is a nail and Castillo has seen a similar nail fastening a horseshoe.

They had beards like yours

They also come from the sky

They rode horses they had lances and swords

They ended two of us with a lance

They went into the sea

They put their lances under the sea

They rode overland away

We saw them ride until dusk

From the place of the buckle and the nail the four men and the rout of guides and hundreds hold a pace headed southward with the South Sea on their right hand sides. Then here the land is become deserted even though it is dark and fertile and rivers run through and ditches carry water into the once planted fields now overgrown and the houses many have been burned and there are stakes in the ground for keeping horses to a place and broken gourds and the people fled.

It was then into the cleft of a mountain to climb nearly upright paths into the cliffs them all thin and scrambling upward to a place where the emaciated fled have gathered to be clear of the men on horseback. Maize as a gift is handed to the arrivals and these loads of maize are handed back to the wasted people who brought the four men here.

Soon departing the mountain retreat the four men bring all those from the mountain southward for none of them could be convinced to return to their homes and four messengers were sent ahead to find what was ahead. On the path southward are signs in each done village, stakes set into the ground and the deep curve of horseshoes into the dirt and the people fled and the fields untended the homes here and there charred.

And then ahead the messengers are only hours in advance of Cabeza de Vaca and his men and the hundreds and the messengers have come upon the camp of the horses and the Christians. The messengers hold a blind behind a thick growth and watch from hidden leaves the Christians. There is a fire and a roasted thing above it. There are horses and Christians upon horses dancing to the nervous step of the horses and the Christians are sworded and helmeted and some have a pike or lance and then a horse who carries a Christian turns his horse head toward the messengers hidden there and chuffs into his deep horse nostrils to smell what is there and the Christian turns his horse toward the hidden messengers and another turns with him and they ride toward the thick growth.

The beat of horses and the sound of armor and swords,
bridles and creaking tack the horses pounding the earth.

Behind the horses men and women some naked some in
deer hides their long oiled black wild hair now dark grass
blown downward their dark eyes wide them all in chains.

ACKNOWLEDGEMENTS

Thank you Gordon Lish.

Thank you David McLendon for your edits, your ear, your conviction.

Thank you Michael Kimball and Leigh Newman for your assistance on early versions of the manuscript.

I would also like to thank Rolena Adorno and Patrick Charles Pautz for their translation of and scholarship on *The Narrative of Cabeza de Vaca*.

Parts of this book were originally published in *Unsaid Magazine* and *3:AM Magazine*.

ABOUT THE AUTHOR

Russell Persson lives in Reno, Nevada. His work has appeared in *The Quarterly, Unsaid Magazine* and *3:AM Magazine*. He is the 2014 recipient of *Unsaid*'s Ivory-Billed Woodpecker Award for Fiction in the Face of Adversity.